THE AURORAL CONTINGENCY

Thom Tate

ASIN: 978-1-0882-5023-5
ISBN-13:

Disclaimer

This book is a work of fiction. Names, characters, places, and incidents either are the product of the author's imagination or are used fictitiously, and any resemblance to any actual person, living or dead, business establishments, events, or locals is entirely coincidental.

Without limiting the rights under copyright reserved above, no part of this publication may be reproduced, stored in, or introduced into a retrieval system, or transmitted in any form or by means (electronic, mechanical, photocopying, recording, or otherwise) without prior written permission of the author.

The scanning, uploading, and distribution of this book via the Internet or via any other means without the express written consent of the author or copyright owner is illegal and punishable by law. Please support your independent authors and purchase only authorized electronic and printed editions. Do not participate in or encourage piracy of copyrighted materials. Your support is appreciated.

Foreword

This book represents the culmination of my dedication and growth as a writer. Throughout this process, I've come to appreciate how an author's style can evolve and their writing can elevate to new heights. The compulsion to revisit and refine previously published works can be irresistible at times. I owe immense gratitude to my dear friend and fellow author, Henry Martin, whose unwavering support and encouragement propelled me to strive for excellence and persevere until the very end. I wholeheartedly recommend delving into his captivating literary creations. Some of his published titles include *Element 115 & Sanctuary in Shadows*.

1

Petrovich Research Facility
   Eastern Siberia, Russia
   December 11th
   15:30 Local Time (07:30 GMT)

The snowmobile launched off a wind-blown bank of snow and soared through the air. Agent Lance Tucker shifted his weight on the machine, negotiated a perfect landing, and gunned the engine. Not all of his six pursuers were able to clear the same mound successfully and continue their pursuit.

He glanced back and grinned with a feeling of satisfaction.

Two down. Four more to go.

A light snow fell as automatic weapons and the screaming of engines ripped through the once serene landscape. Lance tensed and prepared for the worst. Bullets peppered the terrain all around him as he dodged and weaved toward a dense line of trees at the forest's edge. It lay a few hundred yards ahead, and he aimed for the closest opening.

I can lose them in the woods.

The windscreen starred as one of his pursuer's slugs tore through the fabric in his coat, narrowly missing his elbow. The ground flattened out, and Lance reached into his heavy white garment and pulled out his sidearm. With his right hand on the throttle, he turned back over his left shoulder and fired three rounds. The bouncing made it difficult to steady his arm. A single lucky shot found its mark in the chest of the leading pursuer, and he hunched over and fell off his sled.

The second in line plowed into the body and lost control. Lance smiled. From his mirror, the rider dove off and rolled. The abandoned snowmobile capsized and slammed into a boulder, disabled from the chase.

That's two more.

He steered into the tall pines at maximum power, eyes wide with fear as projectiles whizzed past him. He thought back to what Marshal had told him about getting caught. An uneasy feeling crept over him. The fear pumped adrenaline through his veins.

Bark from the trees exploded and bounced off his thick winter coat as the flying lead penetrated the forest surrounding him. Lance looked in front of him and scanned the landscape, searching for the best route to make his escape. He changed his heading to an outcropping of rock to his three o'clock.

Beyond the stone was a clearing. A road was visible. It led out into the vast area known as Siberia. As he sped along, he maneuvered his machine toward the rocks when another barrage of gunfire came his way. Four bullets struck his ride, and a fifth hit his right calf.

Oh Shit! I've been hit. Dammit. Oh, God. I've got to lose them.

Screaming and wincing in pain, he trudged forward. The motor sputtered, and he turned to look behind him as two men on snowmobiles entered the woods to his rear.

It struggled, smoking from the damage. He made a desperate attempt to find a place where he could take cover. He panned left, then opposite. The speed of each breath increased while his engine choked and oil spewed out of the side. In his futile effort to keep his sled moving, his right runner slipped under the fallen branch, hidden in the fresh white powder. The sudden halt flipped him over the machine onto his back.

Lance tried to get up, but the pain emanating from his calf was too intense. Out of desperation, he fired five more rounds at the group of pursuers. He crawled to a mature pine tree and hid out of view from the people who were hunting him.

As he inspected his leg, the wound remained concealed beneath the thick fabric of his pants, however; the blood had already seeped through, staining it a deep red.

Two snowmobiles rejoined the hunt, and all four came to a stop, shy of where his ride lay wrecked. One of them spoke on the radio. It crackled as the response came back.

In the distance, the sound of something bigger resonated through the trees. Panic started to flow through him.

What in the hell is that?

Two minutes later, a snowcat plowed through the woods; its tread gears rattled and squeaked as the cracking of small branches snapped under the weight of the heavy machine.

He peeked around the tree and witnessed more men, along with a pack of dogs, get out of the metal beast. Nikoli Petrovich, the man he had come to acquire information about, was one of those individuals. The canines drowned out the words of people speaking in Russian as they barked, snarled, and fought against their restraints.

"We know where you are, Agent Tucker. The tracks in the snow give you away."

How the hell do they know my name?

"Well, come and get me then!"

"I know you've been shot. You're bleeding! Come out and we can treat you."

Lance closed his eyes and took a deep breath. He pulled the magazine out of his pistol and checked the number of remaining rounds. His left hand slammed it back into the butt of his weapon.

"Yeah? Not a chance."

He spun around the base of the tree, squeezed the trigger, and emptied his gun. The front light on one of the snowmobiles disintegrated as the lead tore through it.

Men on either side of Petrovich ducked for cover, while he stood stoic.

He released the empty mag and inserted a full one as it fell. Bullets penetrated the back of the tree and surrounding snow. Pieces of bark peppered the ground where he sat.

Petrovich raised his hand. "Hold your fire!"

Lance leaned against the trunk. As he exhaled into the frigid air, he couldn't help but track the wisps of his breath dissipating between the skeletal trees around him.

Petrovich shifted his weight as his patience began to wane. "Agent

Tucker. I will release the dogs if you do not come out."

Reality was setting in for Lance. He had screwed up. Tendrils of fear wove their way through him.

Send in the dogs? I don't want to get mauled.

"Who am I talking to?"

"You know perfectly well, Agent Tucker. Do not play me for the fool."

The barking became more constant. They fought against their restraints.

"Yeah—I know who you are. Nikoli Petrovich. The man who wants to *change the world.*"

Nikoli smiled and chuckled. "See? Not so difficult, was it? Now come out and we can treat your wound."

"Fuck you!"

The smile vanished from his face as Petrovich waved his hand forward and signaled to send in the dogs. Two pairs of German Shepherds raced in his direction. Lance raised his firearm, but then they disappeared from view.

Where are those fucking things?

He scanned around the trees, hoping to catch a glimpse of them. It was clear they were there, but hidden.

"Last chance, Agent Tucker."

He shut his eyes and inhaled, feeling the frigid air sting his lungs. The silence unsettled him, sending shivers down his spine.

Without warning, two animals appeared on his right, moving fast. He lifted his weapon to fire, but they made small targets, wide apart. He fired two rounds at the incoming canines. Both shots missed.

As he squeezed the trigger for another shot, something hit him from his left.

Ninety pounds of muscle and bone, traveling at thirty miles per hour, slammed into his side, and jaws clamped down on his shoulder. Close to three thousand joules of energy knocked him flat on his back.

Even as he fell, another dog rammed into him, and a vice tightened on his gun arm. He screamed in pain. A third animal sank its fangs into his thigh, and a fourth grabbed his other ankle.

By this time, he was in excruciating agony as the dogs tried to rip him apart, snarling, pulling, and shaking. The blood flowing from his bites fueled their ferocity, and their attack became ever more savage. His muscles were tearing. He could only scream. This was no way for a man to die.

Powerful jaws shook him like a rag doll, ripping through his clothes and his flesh. His screams shattered the quiet, and the fresh white powder turned to red as he bled from his arms and lower limbs.

Without a hint of concern, Petrovich spun around to the man in charge of the dogs. "Call them off."

Four men raced towards him, each one yelling and grabbing a dog. "*Nyet. Otpustit!*" The animals ignored them, refusing to let go, continuing to shake and tear his flesh. Finally, choking, they released their grip, and the handlers got them on their leashes.

They stood on their hind legs barking like crazy, teeth bared, lunging at him as well as dripping foam and saliva, as the soldiers tried to haul them away from him.

One of them slipped its chain, broke loose and ran back at him, snarling. He was powerless to protect himself, and the beast sank its canines into his crotch.

The handler pulled and yanked at the dog, but it refused to let go. It ripped off a huge chunk of his pants along with tender portions of his anatomy. He prayed for death.

Petrovich approached him with slow, deliberate steps, casting a long shadow over the prone man. His eyes traveled to the crimson stains blossoming across Lance's clothes, a vivid contrast to the pale winter sky above.

Lance's eyes met his. His voice was a hoarse whisper. "You're not going to get away with this. I've reported everything."

"On the contrary, Agent Tucker. I *am* getting away with it." Petrovich reached into his coat and pulled out a Makarov pistol. "And you've not disclosed anything damaging about my operation. We've been watching you."

The man laughed. "We've been spying on the spy." The surrounding men joined in with laughter.

Lance glanced around and weighed his options. His mind raced, calculating every possible phrase capable of swaying his captors and keeping him alive for another moment.

"I've got information. If I don't report back—"

Taking aim at Lance's head with his firearm, Petrovich squeezed the trigger without a shred of hesitation.

As the deafening shot echoed across the snowy terrain, a gory canvas of bone and brains decorated the pristine white snow behind the dead agent.

Petrovich stared out beyond the clearing and through to the road where a lone automobile had stopped. The tiny motor reverberated through the trees. As he tried to focus on it, the vehicle accelerated. He stepped through the snow to his right-hand man, Vasily.

The massive bald man cleared his throat. "What do you want us to do with him?"

Petrovich still focused on the road. "Leave the body for the wolves." He pointed to the vehicle speeding off. "And find out who owns that car."

2

Middleburg, VA
December 12th
01:45 PM

\#

Blake MacKay pulled into the fuel station to refuel and grab something warm to drink. His body was still acclimating to the cold winter air after spending the past few weeks in the perfect middle eastern climate. After returning from an assignment outside of Marea in Syria, he was enjoying some free time.

From time to time, the CIA and the Navy SEALS ran joint missions, and more times than not, they chose Blake to go along. His leadership and fighting skills most closely matched those of America's finest warriors. He had also trained with the various SEAL teams, and he knew the men well.

This time the SEALs mission was to take out the number two and three leaders of ISIS in the region. Their primary task was to help the Kurdish-led Syrian Democratic Forces fight the Islamic State. Once they gathered the intel they needed, they called in the coordinates and the U.S. MQ-9 drones did the rest of the work.

Only returning the previous day, he decided to take some well-deserved time off. Blake's farm was twenty miles from the center of Langley, Virginia, and he planned to stay home most of the time and finish a few projects he had to put on hold.

Blake inserted his credit card and started pumping gas into his Jeep. Finished, he went inside to buy a couple of snacks. After paying the clerk, he stepped outside. There was some unusual movement behind a ratty white van to his left. The yelling male voice caused him to pause.

"Dammit! I told you, you stupid bitch, Milwaukee's Best, not Old Milwaukee Light!"

"I'm sorry baby. I'll—"

"Shut the fuck up! You can't do anything right!"

There was the recognizable sound of a hand striking a face, followed by a female grunting in pain. Blake sidestepped and flanked the van until he could see who was on the other side. A man with scraggly, shoulder-length hair, wearing a black winter coat and grease-stained pants, stood over a brown-haired woman in her early thirties. With clenched fists and his arm cocked, he readied himself to hit her again.

Sitting on the concrete, her knees protruding through the holes in her faded jeans. The dingy white sweatshirt was the only protection she had from his strikes as she raised her arms in defense. "Get up, you dumb bitch!"

The guy struck her as she pleaded with him not to. "No! Please!"

Blake had seen enough. The bag of snacks slid through his fingers and fell to the ground. "Hey! You!"

Before long hair could turn around, Blake ran and pushed him from behind. The man lurched forward onto the pavement. He hustled to his feet and came at his unexpected attacker.

"You need to mind your own business." As he prepared to throw a strike, Blake punched him in the face.

His eyes went wide with surprise. He rubbed his nose and checked for blood. Smiling while he nodded, Blake stood in a boxing stance and egged him on. "Yep, I hit back. Not what you expected, is it, you piece of white trash?"

The guy spat on the ground. "Yeah? You think you're a slick bastard, huh?"

The man reached around to his back.

Oh shit. Please don't pull a gun on me.

As he pulled his hand out, the unmistakable shape unfolded before Blake's eyes. The man held a .38 revolver and pointed it at him. "You don't know who you're messin' with, you dumb terrorist-looking son of a bitch."

Blake chuckled, then laughed. "Terrorist? If you only knew."

The man stepped over to the woman, who whined and pleaded with him. "Randy! Don't."

"Yeah, Randy. It's a terrible idea. You need to think this through."

The guy shook the weapon for emphasis. "Shut up!"

Holding his gaze, and the gun on Blake, he reached to grab her. "Get up! Get up!"

She worked her way to her feet. "Get in the van!"

"But Randy."

"I said get in the goddamn van!"

Blake waited for her to do as he said, so she'd be out of harm's way when he beat the shit out of Randy. His next three moves were already playing through his mind. All he needed was an opening, and he'd strike fast and unforgiving.

His assailant had his back to the vehicle, and he was breathing in short, rapid breaths. Blake could tell he was nervous. The woman closed the door, and he twisted his head left to yell at her again. "Lock the door."

Blake struck as soon as Randy turned. Using a two-handed move he learned from his training, he slapped the firearm out of his assailant's hands and jabbed him in the throat with his four fingers. Randy coughed and tried to raise his hands to his neck.

In a blink, Blake spun and let fly with a fierce kick to his chest. The man flew back and crashed against the van, knocking the wind out of him. His face was white with fear and his eyes were wide with surprise as he stumbled forward.

Blake stepped in and threw his weight behind the final blow, slamming his right elbow into the man's forehead. Randy wilted to the ground, his arms sticking straight out. A display showing the strike was quick and violent, knocking him out cold.

After seeing his opponent sprawled out, he strode over to the weapon, grabbed it, and tucked it into the back of his pants. He moved over to the van's open window, where the woman was dipping her chin in shame.

"Hey."

She didn't talk. There was plenty of evidence of past bruises and half-healed cuts on her body. "Ma'am? He's not going to hit you again." Reaching into his pocket, he pulled out his phone. "I'm calling the police."

She turned and gripped the door frame. "No! No. Don't do it, please."

Blake shook his head. "No. Ma'am, listen to me. The cops are going to come and take him away. I am—"

The door let out an eerie creak as it swung open, as if it were begging for a generous application of lubricant. She stepped toward Blake with outstretched arms, attempting to grab his mobile. Panic in her voice. "No. Gimme the phone."

He batted her arm away as he retreated. "Hey! Stop it! What's wrong with you?"

He dialed 911 and put the phone to his ear. "Even if you won't file charges. I will. The fool assaulted me and brandished a firearm. If I had to guess, he doesn't have a permit for it."

The police answered and while he spoke to them; he observed the woman acting strange and nervous. She would dart a glance at Randy, then back at the van and out over the road, then back to Blake. She was wringing her hands and mumbling.

"Hold on officer."

"Ma'am, are you all right?"

She continued to wring her hands and mumbled under her breath. "No, no, no. I can't do this. I gotta go. No, oh shit!"

"Ma'am?"

She turned and ran to the other side of the van and got into the driver's seat. Blake lifted the phone to speak. "You have the location. Get here now." He shoved the phone in his pocket, lunged for the passenger door, and opened it. She started the engine.

He dove in and latched on to her wrists as she attempted to put the van in gear. With his other hand, Blake reached for the keys and switched the ignition off. She began slamming her palms on the steering wheel. "No! I have to get out of here! Now! I can't do this. I can't get caught!" She placed her face in her hands and began crying.

Blake's brow furrowed. "Caught? What the heck are you talking about?"

He was still sprawled across the passenger seat. He angled his head to his left and saw what was in the back of the vehicle.

"Oh—my—God!"

Sirens filled the air. Blake estimated they were less than a minute away. He wiggled himself out of the van and made certain Randy was still unconscious. After scanning the area, he found a length of orange twine on the ground, which he used to tie the man's hands and feet as a precaution.

You sack of shit.

He circled the van to the driver's side and stood next to the window. The woman still had her face in her hands. "I'm not sure what your involvement is in this, but I suggest you cooperate."

She sobbed while she nodded. Two police vehicles rolled in and parked to block the van. Four officers got out and Blake showed his ID. "I'm CIA. I'm the one who called it in."

As he walked to the back of the van, he pointed toward the driver's side door. "Someone secure her and there is another one knocked out on the other side. He pulled a pistol on me." He made eye contact with the other two officers. "You two, with me."

The van's back windows were blacked out from spray paint on the inside. He opened both doors to reveal two girls, tied and gagged. Blake estimated them to be between eleven and thirteen. The police took the couple into custody and sped off. Blake and a female officer remained with the girls until Children's Services arrived. He bought them sandwiches, ice cream, and juice while they waited. They devoured it all.

After taking care of the children, he drove home and pondered about the identities of the girls. Scolding himself for not thinking to ask them while he stayed with them. Were they sisters? Friends? Did they know each other at all? He had a lot of questions that kept running through his mind.

What could have happened to them had he not intervened? When he got home, he fixed himself a steak, cracked open a cold Scotch Ale, and watched some college basketball. While making a mental note of the things he wanted to accomplish around his farm during his time off, his phone rang.

He glanced at the caller's ID.

What the hell? Why is he calling me?

It was Blake's handler and Director of Clandestine Services at the CIA, Mike Brennan. "You do know I'm on vacation, right?"

"For fuck's sake. You're not home twenty-four hours and you save two kidnapped girls?"

Blake peeked at his watch as he took a swig of his beer. "It's not been five hours. How the fuck did you find out?"

Laughter came from the phone. "You can't be serious. You do know I'm a director at the CIA? It's my job to know *everything* going on with my people."

"Do you know when I take a shit?"

"I can make it happen. And you know it's true."

Blake stood and walked to his kitchen. He held his phone to his chin with his shoulder while he retrieved another beer and opened it. "No. Sorry, I asked."

They both chuckled.

"Listen, I won't keep you. I know this is your time off. However, I need you to come in tomorrow for perhaps an hour. I have a few things to discuss with you and they can't wait. And, knowing you, you're going to want to know about those two girls you saved today, and I'll have a detailed update on them at the same time."

He replied as he walked back to his living room. "Sounds okay. I'll see you in the morning."

#

The next morning, Blake woke early and went for a five-mile run. Joy filled his heart to see horses in his fields once again. Along the route, he made mental notes of the few boards on his fence line, in need of some attention.

Letting the water warm up in his shower, he stood before his mirror. Three weeks in the Syrian sun had turned his already tan complexion darker. His beard had grown out to blend in with the population. He turned his head from one side to the other.

Yeah, I can understand why that asshole called me a terrorist.

He laughed to himself and retrieved his razor from the drawer. After getting dressed and eating, he drove to the CIA headquarters in Langley, Virginia and strolled to Mike's office, rapping on the door frame. Mike was behind his desk. "Blake! Come in."

He stood and sauntered around his desk to greet him. The short, gruff man with a flattop haircut extended his arm.

Blake reciprocated. "Mike."

They shook hands and Mike gestured for him to have a seat. Blake sat on the leather couch in front of Mike's desk. Behind the desk, several pictures chronicled his handler's career during the Cold War. Over the past few years, Blake had gotten to know Mike well. He wasn't only a terrific boss; he had also become a trusted friend.

There was a photo of his handler accepting an award from Ronald Reagan. At six foot one, Reagan towered over Mike and his five feet, eight-inch frame. For the next thirty minutes, they made small talk, and he also gave his boss an abbreviated summary of his mission in Syria.

Mike scooted his chair back, went to the coffeepot in his office, and refilled his cup. "So, I told you I'd fill you in on those two girls."

Blake shifted his position on the couch. "Yeah. What was it all about?"

Mike set his coffee on his desk and sat in his chair. "Well, it turns out the younger one, she's ten and was abducted from a mall in Maryland a week ago. The other one, she is thirteen and has been missing from Portland for almost two months."

"Maine?"

"Oregon."

"Holy shit! That piece of crap went all the way to Oregon?"

Mike shook his head. "No. This is where it gets quite messy. He was the *buyer*."

Blake frowned. His forehead wrinkled. "The buyer?"

Nodding, Mike took a sip of his coffee. "Yeah, the buyer. I think you uncovered a whole major ring of child sex traffickers. This asshole was going to use them to make kiddy pornography and sell access on the dark web."

His jaw clenched. "The mother fuc—"

"Yeah! But now he's looking at life in prison and he's singing like a canary trying to make a deal. We've got the FBI and U.S. Marshalls involved. We don't have any idea how deep this goes, but they're going to follow it to the end."

"Okay. Well. Fantastic. Please keep me informed of what happens."

"I will, and so you know, the two girls you saved are being reunited with their families today."

"Thanks, Mike." Blake slapped his knees and stood. "Well, time for me to head back to the farm."

"Uh, only one more thing. Not a significant deal—yet. But I want to put it on your radar."

"Okay. What is it?"

"We got a call from a station chief in Russia. They dispatched someone, a young and inexperienced agent, no less." He shook his head. "Fucking dumbass. What a colossal mistake." He sat at his desk. "Anyway, they sent him to observe from a distance. Some guy named— Pesterbitch? Sonovobitch? No. Fuck. Hold on." He scrolled through his emails. "Petrovich. Yeah. Got it. Nikoli Petrovich."

Blake shrugged. "Okay. What's he done?"

"I don't have a fucking clue. But this station chief says his guy is about twenty-four hours late from checking in." Mike made a dismissive wave with his hand. "Probably nothing, but only in case it develops into something. I was told to make you aware. You might have to go and find this kid."

Blake laughed. "Okay. Thanks. Keep me up to date if it evolves into anything. And I'm happy to hear the news about the girls."

He turned and left. Mike called after him as he left his office. "I'll let you know if this Petrovich thing gets any traction."

3

Petrovich Research Facility
   Eastern Siberia
   1 Year Ago
   08:56AM (00:56 GMT)

\#

Fifty feet below the antenna, the humming of the array kicking on echoed throughout the massive underground cavern. As far as the eye could see, florescent tubes reflected off the polished gray floors, punctuated only by regimented rows of concrete columns.

The brightly painted paths in the area looked like interconnected circuits on a board. They helped to navigate the golf carts from one end of the vast expanse to the other.

In the center was an elevated glass-walled control room. From here, they controlled the HAARP and satellites. Nikoli Petrovich paced back and forth behind the wall of monitors. His expensive loafers made almost no sound on the hard, raised floor. On his wrist, a Patek Philippe wristwatch with a golden glitter showcased his success and status.

He continued to glance at his watch.

Another two minutes? How is time moving so fast?

His stomach churned, and he wiped the sweat from the back of his neck with a handkerchief. A spider crawled across the otherwise pristine surface. With no regard for his fancy footwear, he squashed it with extreme prejudice.

"How much longer? Have you verified the calibration calculations? I wanted this done by the top of the hour. We have little time left. No excuses!"

The technician in the white lab coat sitting at a terminal answered without looking. "Yes sir. Everything is on schedule. Three minutes until initiation." His fingers danced along the keyboard as he remained focused on the screens in front of him.

"And the Global Relief rescue team? They should be on standby, ready to roll."

"Affirmative, boss. The solar gathering ships are secure and anchored in Manila harbor. Everyone is waiting for your directions." Turning to the man in charge, he smiled. "Don't worry, we have everything under control."

Nikoli Petrovich was a brilliant entrepreneur and scientist, driven by a desire for money and power. At the age of thirteen, they accepted him at the prestigious Moscow Witte University School of Mathematical and Science Studies. After completing his bachelor's degree in only two years, he then pursued his master's in Natural Sciences at Cambridge.

Nikoli's father, Andrei, was a genius in his own right. He co-founded a bioengineering firm and created many medical products. Yet, after incredible achievements, his partner got greedy and accused him of crimes against the state. The police arrested, tried, and jailed him for espionage. Only one year into his sentence, someone killed him in his cell. The events surrounding his demise remained a mystery.

Petrovich strolled over to the panel controlling the satellites, eyeing each monitor along the way. His stomach was in knots, and he took out a pill case from his pocket. From it, he popped two Xanax, swallowing them with a swig of vodka from his flask. While retrieving his cell phone, he cast a quick peek at the wall clock. Pulling a number from his favorites, he connected the call.

"Good morning, Mr. Petrovich. How may I help you?"

"The puts I have for Sri Lanka. Can you confirm when they expire?"

"Let me find out for you, sir."

"Hurry, please."

The person on the other side typed on a keyboard as he listened. "I have it. Okay, wow. You have sizeable investments with hundreds of companies. Was there one in particular—"

"No. All of them!"

His frustration came through with his gruff answers.

"Sir?"

"Yes."

"It's today. As soon as the markets open there in India."

"And what time is that? I'm in the middle of Siberia."

"A little over an hour."

Nikoli pressed the end button and glanced out over all those working in the room to prepare for the test.

Billions of dollars are on the line. They're all contingent on the auroral array functioning as it should.

Wiping a nervous sweat from his brow, Nikoli shouted out. "All right everyone. This is it."

Pitor was his lead scientist in charge of the High-frequency Auroral Array Research Program (HAARP). Pitor leaned over the central control panel and turned four switches, as well as a yellow knob, which he rotated 180 degrees.

A strange hum filled the room. People all around were monitoring various dials and digital readouts. Petrovich kept his eyes on a live satellite view of the Laccadive Sea. He focused on an area 182 kilometers south of Kanyakumari, India, and 145 kilometers west of Colombo, Sri Lanka.

Pitor shifted his attention to Petrovich. "Everything is looking perfect so far, sir. The satellites are in line and ready."

Petrovich nodded. Pitor raised his hand and pointed to another scientist. "Now."

Petrovich's eyes swept back and forth between the satellite image and the seismic readers, his eyes darting. His nerves were like pinpricks. No change. He took three steps away from the console and then turned back. "How much longer?"

"You need to give it a few minutes. We're pushing to a depth of thirty kilometers below the seabed."

Petrovich eyed the yellow knob. "What's the percentage of power?"

Pitor walked over to the console and glanced at it. "It's at forty percent. The standard amount."

"Go to sixty."

Pitor's eyes widened. "Sir?"

"You heard me. Sixty. Do it now!"

Pitor pressed his lips together and obeyed without saying a word.

With considerable trepidation, he rotated the dial to match his bosses' orders. The humming increased in volume and pitch. The floor had a slight vibration. Petrovich was laser focused on the seismic monitors. They shifted.

"Sixty-five."

Pitor adjusted the dial. The pitch and hum got even louder. The seismic monitors' needles changed, but not enough.

"Seventy-five."

Pitor's gaze shifted to one of his colleagues. They both swallowed hard.

"Seventy-five, God dammit!"

"Yes, sir." A reluctant Pitor rotated the knob. The humming and pitch grew uncomfortable, causing several people to cover their ears. The shaking rattled their teeth, intensifying the quaking vibrations. Petrovich stared at the monitors.

"Dammit! All the way!"

Pitor cupped his hand over his ear. "What? I can't hear you!"

Nikoli stomped over to the control panel, brushed the scientist aside, and cranked the knob all the way to the right. The noise was deafening, and the ground vibrated more. Pitor grabbed Petrovich's arm. "Sir! We've never tested it this high before. We need—"

Petrovich knocked off the unwelcome touch and regarded him with narrowed eyes. His attention returned to the seismic monitors. They registered an earthquake thirty kilometers below the seabed. It was registering a 9.4 on the Richter scale. Early wave-detecting beacons were reporting 30- to 38-foot-tall waves.

A smile formed on Petrovich's face and he motioned for Pitor to cut everything off. Without hesitation, the man turned the yellow knob to zero and flipped off the switches in reverse order. The shaking and noise subsided. Petrovich stepped toward Pitor. "There. Do you see? You have to push limits in order to break them."

Pitor's face was red from the blood rushing to his head out of anger. "Are you fucking crazy? We've nev—"

Petrovich backhanded Pitor, who flew back and onto the floor. Others in the room stopped talking and observed the commotion. Nikoli leaned over and shook an accusatory finger at him. "Shut up! You do not tell me what we can and cannot do. You're weak! Afraid to take risks! You're pathetic."

He slammed his hand on the table nearby. "If you ever dare to repeat such behavior, I'll take you fifty kilometers beyond the gate and leave you." Nikoli stood tall and addressed everyone in the room. Raising his arm, he pointed in a sweeping motion. "And anyone else in here who disobeys my orders will get the same treatment."

Pitor sat on the floor and leaned back on his arms, his cheeks flushed with a rosy hue. He avoided making eye contact and fidgeted with the hem of his shirt. "So, what do we do now?"

Petrovich turned toward Pitor. "Now? We wait."

#

Kudankulam, India

07:35 AM (02:35 GMT)

Darpan Sharma and his eight-year-old son, Avi, completed stocking the shelves at their tiny store in the village of Kudankulam. They opened at 08:00 daily and Avi helped by placing the produce on the outside stands for his father before he walked to school.

Avi ran into the shop and yelled out for his father, who was putting canned goods on a shelf at the back of the cash register. "Pappa, I finished arranging the fruit on the street. Can I go to school now?"

His father stepped off the stool and wiped his hands on his dingy white apron. "You are a fine boy. Have you milked the goats?"

Avi didn't answer. His father came from behind the counter to see what his son was doing. When he spotted the lad's shocked reaction, he grinned and decided to continue his joke. "How are we going to sell fresh milk if you don't milk the goats?"

He reached behind the counter and retrieved a pail. With it dangling from his fingers, he handed it to his son. Avi stood. His brow furrowed, and his lower lip pushed out. "But—pappa."

Darpan laughed and smiled. "I am kidding. I will milk the goats." He placed a loving hand on his son's shoulders. "But this is something you will need to learn soon. Okay?"

Avi returned a grin to his father and nodded. "Yes, Pappa."

His father's smile faded into obscurity.

Avi cocked his head. "What's the matter?"

The faint rumble of the earthquake grew louder until it reached a deafening crescendo, shaking everything in its path. Panic assailed him. "What's happening?"

"Pappa, what's wrong?"

Fear surged through Darpan. Lunging toward his son, he grabbed him and took cover under a table.

Jars and canned vegetables crashed and shattered on the surface. Other goods and produce fell from the shelves and splattered across the floor. Darpan wrapped his arms around Avi and held him close to his chest. White flour from a burst bag filled the air and stuck to their sweaty skin.

The table Avi had arranged outside turned over and fruit rolled onto the dirt street in front of their store.

#

Samantham Towers were twin residential complexes near the Atomic Energy Central School. The earthquake shocked Veda Ray out of a sound sleep, rattled her bed, and sent her plunging into dazed confusion. There was a deafening rumble, as if a herd of stampeding elephants were storming through her home.

The noise of glass shattering, objects sliding off shelves, and screaming penetrating through the thin walls was never-ending. She bolted toward her living room. Paralyzed with fear, Aisha, her roommate, stood in the center of the room wearing her light blue pajamas. "Aisha! What's happening?"

Her eyes met Veda's. She tried to talk, but terror froze her. Veda stumbled onto their balcony to investigate. Blasts from car alarms and horns blared from the parking lot fifteen stories below. Her mouth was agape, her upper lip curling back. Grimacing, she wanted to look away, but it was impossible, and her head recoiled from the source, eyes wide and staring.

The earth shook with incredible violence. Buildings crumbled in the earthquake's wake, and clouds of dust rose into the air like a thick, choking fog. Veda turned back to face her roommate. She was sweating with fear. "Aisha! It's an earthquake!"

The balcony shuddered. As Veda fought to stay on her feet, she witnessed an enormous crack appear and move along the full width of the terrace by the door. She gasped. "Oh, God! No!"

As she pushed herself off the guardrail to run back inside, the balcony broke from its anchor on the building. The rebar in the concrete bent 90 degrees from the weight and was now dangling off the side of the structure. Veda fell backward. The railing, her only savior from death, reached out to her from a hundred and sixty feet below. "Aisha!

Help me!"

Adrenaline pumped through her, giving her the courage she needed to move. Aisha rushed to the balcony opening. "Oh, my God! Veda!"

She lay prone and extended her hand, but it was too far. "I can't reach. I'll find something."

As she rose, a massive shockwave hit the structure. It knocked her back into the apartment on the floor. She stumbled to her feet, desperate to assist her friend. Having stood, she called out. "Veda!"

The balcony, along with Veda, was gone. Aisha turned to her kitchen in disbelief. "Veda! No…"

A lone tear rolled down her cheek. The building collapsed.

#

Alarms screamed. Warning lights flashed. Buzzers were relentless and never-ending. Like listening to every sound in the world at once. Jaret Combs was the managing superintendent for the Kudankulam Nuclear Power Plant. He burst into the central command. "What the hell is going on?"

The shift supervisor, Tarak Patel, stepped toward him. "Cooling towers are offline. It's getting hotter!"

"Shut it down! Do it now! Can somebody tell me what the fuck is happening?"

Tarak followed Jaret to the central terminal. "There's been a nine-point—I don't know, three or four—it doesn't matter. There was an earthquake, a hundred and eighty kilometers off the coast."

Jaret's brow furrowed. "Earthquake? What the hell? There isn't even a fault line there, is there?"

"No, there isn't." Tarak grabbed Jaret's arm to get his attention. "But it gets worse."

Jaret tilted his head and closed his eyes when the realization hit him. "Fukushima! Please don't tell me there is a tsunami heading this way."

Tarak nodded. "Yes. And we have twenty minutes until it hits."

Rubbing the back of his neck, Jaret glanced all around him. People scampered in all directions, trying to get the cooling towers back online. He turned back to Tarek. "We can't do this. We have to evacuate!"

"No! The towers!" Tarek shook his head. "We'll go into full meltdown!"

He placed his hand on Tarek's shoulder. "You let me worry about those towers. Get everyone out of here now."

#

When the waves hit the shores of Colombo, Sri Lanka, hundreds, if not thousands, of buildings crumbled or toppled. Wealthy builders bribed safety inspectors to maximize their profits, making the buildings vulnerable. Seismic shocks destroyed these structures.

The merciless sea first devoured Colombo City Port's Beach Park. It wiped away everything in its path. The next victim was the Yugadanavi Power Plant, which sat one kilometer from the shore. 700,000 people lost electricity. The waves washed over Negombo Lagoon. On its edge lies Bandaranaike International Airport.

The wheels of a Sri Lanka Airlines Boeing 737 aquaplaned, as the waves persevered on their relentless course. The aircraft lurched as the landing gear sped through the water at almost 100 mph. It struck the sea with its port side wing. The plane dipped its nose, rolling once before blowing up and disintegrating,

As the water parade went on, it included bodies, suitcases, and airplane components. For an additional eighteen kilometers inland, the wave of destruction continued its path. The earthquake left a devastating toll of 280,000 missing or dead and 1.7 million without electricity.

#

Jaret wiped the sweat from his brow. He'd been through SCRAM, or emergency shutdown training, and renewed his certificate every year, but the last time was eight months ago. He tried to recall all the steps and necessary precautions.

When the Fukushima plant lost its backup power in the tsunami, it lost the ability to pump water around the nuclear fuel. This prevented the water from acting as a coolant. As a result, the pressure built up, forcing the operators to vent steam and other gases to keep the pressure in check.

Jaret checked the solar generators he would require for back up power. They weren't on. The building shook, and he grabbed his radio. "Tarek. Is everyone out of here?"

"Yes, all are out, except for you. What are you doing?"

The building trembled again. A wave of aftershocks rocked the area, with quakes measuring from 5.5 to 6.8 on the Richter scale. "Starting a SCRAM. I've got to dump these rods into the core, but I need those backup generators online to pump the water in."

"Yeah, I thought you might want those."

A piece of the ceiling slammed into the floor behind Jaret. "Jesus!" He ran to the wall and grabbed a hard hat. He placed it on his head and called out to Tarek on the radio. "Tarek! Where are you? What did you say?"

The building rocked. Small beams and concrete crashed down from above.

"I've got the generators on, but—"

A loud rumble filled the room. Jaret lost his footing and hit the floor. A chunk of concrete glanced on the side of his hard hat and slammed to the floor beside him. Sirens blared, warning of a meltdown. Jaret shook it off and struggled to his feet. Another roll from the ground below. The feeling was the same as walking on a waterbed. He stumbled once more. A steel rod fell from the ceiling. Jaret rolled to his right and glanced up. "No!"

The smooth rod impaled him through his thigh and pinned him to the floor. Panicked, he searched for his radio. It was out of reach. He stretched for it, but the pain in his leg was excruciating. Jaret pulled on the rod and tried to dislodge it from the ground, but failed. The door to the control center flung open. Tarek jumped the four steps and ran toward him.

Jaret shook his head. "No, not me. Not yet. The pumps. Turn on the pumps and hit the SCRAM button!"

Tarek patted him on the back. "Okay, but the wave. I saw it. We have perhaps thirty seconds before it hits us."

A seismic wave rumbled through the building. More debris fell. A huge portion of the roof fell and hit the control panel a few feet from Tarek. It landed on the rocker arm they used to turn on the pumps.

"It's jammed! I can't move it." Grabbing a nearby lump of concrete, he started hammering it.

"No! Stop. Don't do it. You'll break it and we'll be fucked for sure." Jaret motioned with his head. "Over there. Grab the rod over there. Use it as a pry bar."

Tarek ran to the rod. A strange rumbling noise, unlike any they'd encountered before, filled the room. Tarek's and Jaret's eyes met. Both realized together. "Water!"

Water splashed into the room and spilled down the stairs. Tarek placed the pry bar under the rocker arm and pried. Jaret focused on the ever-increasing water level. "Hurry, God dammit!"

"I'm trying!" He gritted his teeth and ground his feet to the floor. Water rushed to his shoes. Debris filled the room. He grunted and pried with all his strength. The rocker moved to the 'on' position. "I got it! I got it!"

In one swift move, he hit the SCRAM button and started an emergency shutdown. The control rods fell into the reactor and ended the fission reaction. Tarek hurried over to Jaret. It was then he understood Jaret's situation. Still pinned to the floor, the water level was now over a foot deep and covering Jaret's legs. Tarek brushed his long black bangs out of his eyes. He crouched beside Jaret. "Oh my God, your leg."

His sweaty hands slid as he attempted to draw the rod. Again, the building shook. More debris landed. The sound of rushing water grew louder. He unzipped the white lab coat from his body and used it to better hold the rod. Getting to his feet, he grasped the rod in both hands and pulled. Jaret squeezed his eyes shut tight and let out a roar. "No, no, no! Oh, holy shit! No! Stop!"

He took several deep breaths. "No." Jaret shook his head. "I'm done. This rod. It's through my bone. I wouldn't be able to swim or tread water if you got it out. You need to get out of here. Get to the top of the building. We're deep into this tsunami now."

The ceiling disintegrated into larger pieces, and more frequent. Jaret handed Tarek his hard hat. The building rocked. Water flow increased. "Go! Get out of here!"

Tarek nodded. The last thing Jaret heard was the splashing of Tarek's steps as he trudged through the water. Another rumble and an enormous chunk of the ceiling landed on Jaret, crushing him.

4

CIA Station
    Moscow, Russia
    November 30th
    07:20 (22:20 GMT Nov 29th)

#

Agent Lance Tucker strode into the Chief of Station's office with an hour to spare before his meeting. Despite being only twenty-four, he exuded the drive of an up-and-coming star. At times, Marshal found Tucker's zeal overwhelming and had to keep reminding him to be patient.

The Chief navigated the washing machines and industrial driers that disguised the retail space's true intent. All the appliances were part of the ruse disguising the true nature of the premises. The location was a dry cleaner, staffed with Chinese Nationalists who were prior CIA assets. They had either finished their mission or became compromised and needed to escape imprisonment or execution from the CCP.

From outside his office, he noticed the youthful agent waiting for him. The hand on the perpetually bouncing knee had a recognizable ring on it. It was an anxious twitch. He'd have to persuade the boy to lose. Julie Maren, one of his more experienced analysts, caught his eye as he groaned.

"For fuck's sake. How long has he been here?"

Julie's eyes shifted up through the top of her hound's tooth reading glasses and focused on Chief Reed.

"When I got here fifteen minutes ago, he was already hanging around outside."

Marshal glanced at his watch. "Our meeting isn't for another forty." After taking a deep breath, he exhaled. "Oh fine. I might as well get this done. I'll be glad to see him gone for a while. Perhaps this will keep him from bugging me."

Julie raised her yellow smiley face mug and gestured as if giving a toast. "Have fun."

His young colleague stood to greet him as he entered the room.

"Good morning, Chief Reed."

After removing his winter coat, he placed it on a hook in the corner and tossed a newspaper onto his desk. With no greetings, he turned to face the youngster.

"Sit down, kid."

Lance obliged with his grin, never leaving his face. Marshal walked back out of the office carrying his empty cup and returned after two minutes had elapsed. As he strolled in, he enjoyed another swig of coffee and plopped himself in his black leather chair.

He scooted forward, clasped his hands, and rested them in front of him. "Ya know—we were supposed to meet at eight o'clock. Remember what I told you about being patient?"

"Oh." Lance stood and his cheeks turned rosy. "I only thought—I mean." The youth motioned with his thumb. "If you wish, I'll return later."

His boss waved it off. "No, no, no. Sit down. You're fine. We'll discuss this now and afterwards; we can both continue with our day."

As he sat, the Chief eyed the junior agent sitting in before him. Well dressed in a dark blue suit, crisp white shirt, and bright green tie. Along with his handsome features, brown, wispy hair covered his forehead. His face was youthful and full of exuberance, lacking the wrinkles and scars from age and experience.

"What did you want to talk to me about, Mr. Reed?"

He shook his head and closed his eyes. "Oh, for fuck's sake, call me Marshal. You make me feel like I'm the principal of some high school and you're some dumb kid in a crisis."

Lance chuckled as his shoulders dropped to relax. His smile lingered. "Ok. I can do that. But—I'm not in trouble, am I?"

Marshal's head moved from side to side as he peered at him. "No, my boy. You're not."

The junior agent made the motion of wiping his forehead and smiled. "Whew."

"Okay. Fine. Now that's over, study this and tell me what you see."

The chief tossed him the newspaper. He unfolded it and scanned over the front page.

Twenty seconds later, Lance turned the paper around to face Marshal. He pointed to a picture. "Are you talking about Nikoli Petrovich?"

The Chief nodded. "Yep."

"I've heard about him. Is there something I should know?"

"You're the analyst. You tell me."

Scanning over the article to see if anything particular stood out. Nothing did. He folded the newspaper and set it on the desk. "I know he's a billionaire. A bit of a philanthropist, isn't he? Oh." He snapped his fingers. "He built that—that thing."

The chief raised his eyebrows. "That thing? Is that all you got? Come on. You want to go out in the field so bad. You've gotta do better than that."

Lance shifted his weight to the front of the chair and straightened his back. "I got it. Gimme a second." He pointed at his boss. "Changes the climate. It can change the weather. Make it rain, baby. That's it." He clapped his hands together as if he'd won the grand prize on a game show. "Whew! Am I correct?"

The Chief lost his fight to suppress a smile. "Yes, you got it right."

His grin was infectious. "Awesome! So, what about it?"

"Okay. Time to get serious." Marshal lifted the remote from his desk and jerked his thumb at an extensive monitor on the wall. The screen displayed a massive bank of towers in an enclosure covering 400 acres. The square had 3600 antennae arranged in an array of sixty by 60.

"This is his ionospheric research instrument. He uses this to disrupt the ionosphere, and they have proven that he can make it rain—sometimes—in areas he can designate. Now, conspiracy nuts have complained for years about the system we have in Alaska, that it can cause tsunamis, hurricanes and earthquakes. Plus, a bunch of other nonsense."

"Can it?"

Marshal turned to face Lance and ignored the question. He shifted his attention back to the screen. Displayed on the monitor was a colorful picture of what appeared to be Earth.

"These are satellite images taken at various times."

He stood, walked over to the screen, and pointed at specific locations. "There has been turbulence in the ionosphere above Petrovich's—thing—as you called it, here and here, following recent natural disasters. We suspect there is some validity to these claims. The infrared satellite images show the disturbance."

He tossed the remote onto his desk and turned to his young operative.

Lance sat in deep thought for a moment before he spoke. He sighed. "It would appear—that this is above my paygrade. Why are you telling me this?"

The chief scratched his right eyebrow and cracked a smile. "You've been pestering me about what it takes to be a field agent." He rubbed his chin and took a sip of his coffee. "You're about to get a crash course."

Lance's broad grin revealed his infectious enthusiasm, highlighted by a brilliant set of pristine white teeth. "I am?"

Marshal raised both hands, palms facing the boy. "Now hold on there, cowboy. This is a watch and observe mission, only. Only! I can *not* emphasize that enough. Watch and observe—from an extremely *safe* distance. OFD, put that in your list of acronyms to remember. Observe from a distance."

Lance nodded. "I can do that."

"Yeah, well, when you get the details of this, you'll change your mind about working in the field. You've heard about getting sent to Siberia as a punishment. Well, that ain't no shit."

He handed the enthusiastic young man a mission packet. It was a sealed white envelope with red markings around the edge. There was a "Classified" stamp in the center.

"Don't bother opening it. That's for later. I'll tell you what's in there."

"Okay." Lance sat back in his chair and listened with the rapt attention of a diver preparing to plunge into uncharted depths.

"First off, I need to tell you that you're going to get to put your jump school skills to the test. We're going to parachute you in twenty-five kilometers from his compound. We'll drop a snowmobile and supplies with you. You'll make camp ten klicks from there, and that will be your base of operation."

He leaned over and shook his finger. "Safety is paramount. Do you comprehend? Among some of the tech goodies you'll have are infrared, night vision, parabolic microphones and a lot of other tools you can use to observe and collect data—safely—from a distance. I know I mentioned that before, but Lance, I can't emphasize it enough. Do not take any action of any kind. This is a fact-finding mission only. Do you understand?"

He nodded. "Yes, I follow all that, and—"

Marshal raised his hand to cut him off.

"Nope. Hold on. Allow me to drive home how severe this is, because, son, let me tell you. You're going to be three-thousand miles away. It's going to be fucking freezing, too. Like thirty below, so you need to have your shit together."

His brows pinched in a frown. "There is nobody—not a soul—anywhere. That can come to your rescue. If they discover you, you will disappear into the deepest hell of hells in their prison system. And that's only if they don't kill you on sight."

The chief glanced at the kid, studying his reaction to the news he had shared.

"So young man. You still up for this?"

Lance stood. "Yes, sir. I understand. I can do this. Thank you for this opportunity."

"All right. Extraction info will be in the packet. Don't open that until you get on the plane. Best of luck."

"Uh, Sir? I mean Marshal."

"Yeah."

"When do I go?"

"Now! Get the fuck outta here. Go."

He turned to leave when Marshal intercepted him. "Wait." He opened his desk drawer, retrieved a cell phone, and tossed it to him. "You're going to need that. You'll get instructions on who to meet and when to get out of there."

Marshal followed him out of his office and halted next to Julie's desk.

She took off her glasses and shifted to face her boss. "Why are we not sending any of the other field agents?"

"Want me to be honest?" He sipped his coffee. "They didn't want to go. Too fucking cold."

#

10 kms from Petrovich's Research Facility

Siberia

December 11th

Lance sat in his tent and scrolled through the hours of audio recordings he'd made over the past ten days. When he parachuted in, they had also dropped two pallets of equipment. One contained an all white Yamaha Sidewinder L-TX LE. A high-performance sled that produced over 200 horsepower and enough fuel to outlast his intended stay.

They retrofitted it with a unique muffler, ensuring it was as quiet as the electrical equivalent, which wouldn't work in such extreme cold. The other included his tent, cold weather gear, food, water, heaters, other supplies, and a standard-issue Glock with plenty of ammunition.

On the plane ride over, He studied basic schematics of the area and mapped out where he would place the parabolic microphones. He placed them away from electrical components and where he thought Petrovich would have the most access.

During the flight, they implanted a small pellet under his skin and installed an application on his phone. They instructed him how to transfer any intelligence he had gathered to the capsule. Later, they could extract that data for review in the event his telephone or laptop became compromised.

The past ten days had yielded little in the way of recordings. He soon realized the electrical interference the array created was going to be problematic. Trying to listen through thick concrete walls was difficult enough, but the added intrusion resulted in recordings of poor quality.

He also learned that Petrovich soundproofed his office, so he abandoned all efforts at collecting recordings there.

Lance earmarked only a few recordings he deemed as *interesting,* or a *potential piece* to the puzzle. He listened to them again to transcribe to text files.

Recording 6 December 3rd: Unknown person 1: "*unintelligible gibberish* of the array. Petrovich put *unintelligible* full power. *unintelligible gibberish* Fukashima *unintelligible, unintelligible* next test.*"

Unknown Person 2: "Right. And the last *unintelligible gibberish*.... Success."

Recording 4 December 8th: Unknown Person 1: "It's been almost a year *unintelligible gibberish* tested the array. Sri Lanka got it the worst, I think."

Unknown Person 2: "I don't know, the *unintelligible* nuclear plant got wiped out. Do we know *unintelligible gibberish* target *unintelligible* next test?"

Unknown person 1: "*unintelligible gibberish.* ber 21st."

He noted those as having the most interesting and revealing information. He decided to listen to the recordings from yesterday before reviewing the others. The first four proved to be like most of the others, gibberish and nothing that he could decipher. But it was the fifth one that jolted him and set his adrenaline racing.

Recording 5 December 11th: Unknown person 1: "Mister Petrovich, *unintelligible*, for a moment?"

Perhaps Petrovich: "Yes."

Unknown person 1: "*unintelligible* for the next test on the 21st. I know you had several targets in mind. *unintelligible* ...alse, Argentina, Angra One, Brazi.. *gibberish* ...an Diego or Oslo?"

Petrovich: "Oslo. Save San Diego for the 25th. *Unintelligible* Christmas gift they'll never forget."

"Oh, my God!"

I've got to do something. My extraction date isn't for another week. Do I do something? Marshal said this was observation only. If I call it in, they'll tell me not to do anything. By the time they get someone here, it will be too late.

He opened the schematics of the compound. There was little knowledge about the interior of the place. However, he discovered the point where they piped natural gas into the building from outside.

He combed through the gear they supplied him. He gathered his Glock and loaded several spare magazines. As he searched, he came across a box.

What's this?

Inside was a stack of square explosive patches, four by 4 inches. These were peel-and-stick explosives that could attach to almost anything and detonated by remote. Lance turned back to the schematic on his laptop and focused on the two gas mains.

That's it!

Using his training, he layered his clothing and finished with his all white pants and parka. He grabbed a stack of the explosive patches and zipped them into his jacket pocket.

He rode the sled to the top of a ridge. Halfway down the hill, he noticed an outcropping of rock that would be useful to hide the sled behind. He estimated the gas mains to be a half-klick walk from there. A chain-link fence with cameras facing both in and out of the perimeter surrounded the building.

After he parked the ski, he proceeded to another smaller clump of rocks. From there, he could monitor the eastern side of the building, as well as the north face where his target was located.

Using his binoculars, he timed their rotation and when the cameras didn't point in his direction. They moved at varying speeds, and there would be times when they would capture him.

His two weeks of observation allowed him this knowledge, so he brought the camera jammer that had been a part of his supplies. It sent interruption-code frequencies in the 900MHz to 2499MHz range and would allow him to move without being detected by the cameras. After configuring the jammer, Lance proceeded to the fence.

He cut through the linkage with his utility tool and slid through the opening. The gas mains were fifty meters from the fence. He hurried to the first and stuck a detonator patch on it and moved to the next. His heart raced as he pulled back the adhesive cover. Pushing a small button embedded in the center of the patch, he watched as a tiny LED light glowed red.

He was all too happy to put his gloves back on. It was below freezing, and light snow began falling.

Okay. They're armed.

He opened the app on his phone and saw the red lights that represented each explosive patch. They connected via an encrypted Bluetooth connection that had an extended range of up to 500 meters.

Trusting the technology, but being extra cautious, he waited until both cameras were facing away from his line of escape. When they were, he made his move. He slid back out through the hole in the fence and ran toward the first outcropping. On his phone, he opened the schematic. He made notes of where he placed the explosives. The information automatically transferred to the capsule.

Youth, inexperience, and over-confidence got the best of him. Without thinking, he forgot to check his surroundings and started running for the sled when he heard from a distance.

"Vy tam! Ostanavlivat'sya! Vernut'sya syuda!"

Lance turned. Two armed guards were running toward him. In the distance, the unmistakable buzzing of snowmobile engines filled the air.

Oh shit!

His heart raced. He sprinted for the next outcropping his sled was behind. He heard again.

Vy tam! Ostanavlivat'sya! Vernut'sya syuda!

His mind translating.

You there! Stop! Come back here!

Bullets ricocheted off the top of the rocks.

He started his saving grace and as he accelerated away, a quick glance over his shoulder revealed six men on snowmobiles in quick pursuit.

5

Petrovich Research Facility
   Eastern Siberia, Russia
   December 14th
   09:10AM (01:10 GMT)

#

Twenty-nine-year-old Sofia Kuzma walked into her office. Today started out like any other. After placing her cup of tea on her desk, she reached over and turned on her computer. During the time it took to boot, she hung her coat on the rack which stood in the corner. Then, as part of her daily routine, she opened her calendar and checked the tasks she had to complete.

Growing up poor in Moscow, she was the third of four children and was the only girl. She had a close relationship with her mom, despite having been ignored by her father. Memories of their time together while being taught how to cook and sew were some of the few she cherished.

A smile brightened her features as she reminisced about how her mother nagged about the value of honing her household and cooking skills. Her mother always said they would help her in finding a decent man.

Sofia interpreted it to mean she wasn't worth anything unless she performed well in home economics. It left her feeling as if no one had confidence in her abilities. She realized at a young age, applying herself to her schoolwork was the only way to be successful and break free from Moscow.

Her hard work paid off with a scholarship to the prestigious Russian New University. After graduating top of her class, she received more scholarships for a higher degree. She selected Cambridge, where she earned her doctorate in meteorology with honors.

Solid employment after school proved difficult. Despite having ample qualifications, most companies turned her away for being 'over-qualified'. Thankfully, a stroke of luck led her to a meteorologist's position at a local broadcast station in Moscow. Her job involved forecasting the regional weather.

Her opportunity was perhaps because of her blond hair, high cheekbones, and piercing green eyes, rather than her education. The station's hiring manager tried his best to sleep with Sofia as a requirement for landing the position. A quick kick to the balls and a lie that her brother worked for the FSB and would have him jailed soon halted him in his tracks.

Nevertheless, it was a job. She turned out to be the most popular 'weather girl' on television. Her stunning looks attracted the attention of many male viewers.

Nikoli Petrovich discovered her while she was doing a broadcast. In a rare moment, the workaholic was decompressing from a twenty-hour workday when he switched on the news. Her beauty was striking. Reading her professional profile on the company's website more than impressed him. They had both attended the same university, which made her even more appealing to him. He called the TV station and arranged a meeting.

When they met, he explained how he was developing an array similar to HAARP, the High-Frequency Active Auroral Research Program, implemented in the United States. It was an amazing technology, enabling him to control the climate.

His ambition was to bring rain to drought-torn areas of Africa as a means for villages to grow their own food and help to eliminate world hunger. He spoke of his other philanthropic organizations, which immediately impressed her.

She jumped at the opportunity. The last thing she wanted to be was a 'weather girl' and another cute face on the television. She had a deep desire to do something meaningful with her life.

Vasily, Nikoli's personal assistant, or bald henchman, as others at the facility called him, walked into her office unannounced. He was wearing the same black suit and tie he always wore. She wondered if he had a whole closet of suits or only one.

"Miss Kuzma, Mr. Petrovich would like a word with you, please. Come now?"

She glanced away from her computer monitor and pointed to herself. "Mr. Petrovich wants to see me?"

"Yes. Hurry. he doesn't like to be kept waiting."

Although they had spoken during earlier meetings, Petrovich had never extended an invitation to his workspace. The billionaire's office was rumored to be extremely lavish, but she had never seen it in person.

The timing, however, couldn't have been worse. With a major test approaching, he tasked her with getting the entire array online and testing it prior to the deadline. Previous tests were only partial and did not include the array's full potential.

Sofia entered Petrovich's office with Vasily close behind. It was perhaps bigger than her lab. Beautiful parquet floors covered the room. A huge marble fireplace decorated the far side of the room with an orange fire burning. Petrovich interrupted her gaze as she tried to take it all in.

He smiled and spread his arms in a welcoming manner. "Ah, Miss Kuzma. Welcome to my workplace. Can I get you some coffee?"

"Tea please, one sugar."

Nikoli snapped his fingers and Vasily exited the room. He motioned for Sofia to take a seat in one of the overstuffed chairs sitting in front of his desk. Nikoli remained standing and leaned back against his mahogany desk.

She scanned the billionaire from head to toe. He was attractive, with dark hair and eyes. His complexion was too pale for her tastes, but it didn't take away from his handsome features. His fit for fashion was tasteful, with black pleated pants and alligator loafers. He topped it off with a loose-fitting button-down shirt. She didn't know what kind of watch he wore, but it appeared expensive.

"Miss Kuzma—can I call you Sofia?"

Her mouth curved into a smile and she recalled their first meeting. He was as charming now as he was then. "Yes. Of course."

Nikoli's eyes gleamed, and he crossed his arms. "How is the array coming? We have the test in a couple of weeks, and I want to make sure we are on schedule. Do you require anything?"

"No, there's nothing I need. Everything is on track. You will be pleased to hear we're ahead of schedule and it should be well ready to go."

He uncrossed his arms and clasped his hands. "Brilliant, it is indeed excellent news." Nikoli walked toward the fireplace. Vasily entered the room and handed Sofia her tea.

She grasped the mug. "Thank you."

Vasily moved back a few feet and stood over her like a guard dog.

A tiny pucker of a frown crossed Nikoli's face. "I have a strange question for you. Was it your vehicle I saw on the road leaving the facility yesterday?"

Her brow scrunched and her lips pouted as she considered. "Uh…" She set the cup on the table.

Petrovich stepped toward her. "Stopped—not far from the security gate?"

Her frown of concentration disappeared as she recalled. "Oh. Yes, of course, you did."

How would he know what kind of car I drive?

"What were you doing? You know we don't allow cars to stop along there."

"The blower motor for my heater wasn't working, and I was searching for my gloves. It was cold inside."

Nikoli rubbed his chin while his eyes focused on hers. "Oh dear, how—unfortunate. You know, Vasily here is excellent at fixing things. Perhaps you can pull it into the garage, and he can repair it for you."

"Well." She took a sip of her tea and placed it back on the table next to her chair. "I appreciate the offer, but," a broad grin spread across her face. "I fixed it myself."

"You did?" Nikoli cocked his head and his dark brows raised. "And what did you do to fix it?"

Sofia couldn't resist a smile. "It was the fuse. I did a little research on the internet when I got home. Quick and easy."

Nikoli nodded and smiled. "You are resourceful, Miss Kuzma."

"Thank you." She glanced over at Vasily, who stood emotionless.

Something in her mind told her not to ask the next question, but curiosity got the best of her.

"How did you know I stopped? Are there cameras there?"

Nikoli shook his head and reached for the fire poker. "No. No, we don't need them out here. We were out in the woods." He bent and gave a log a forceful poke.

Sofia cocked her head to the side and scrunched her brow. "The woods? Well, whatever for?"

He stood and replaced the fire poker. He pivoted back to face her. "Wolves."

"Wolves?"

Sofia placed her hand over her mouth and glanced at Vasily and back to Petrovich.

"Are we safe? Do we have to worry about those things?"

"Yes, you are protected. Some men who patrol the perimeter fence at night have reported seeing them. We want to make sure everyone is secure, so we went on a little hunting expedition."

Nikoli clasped his hands and stepped toward her. "Well, I guess that's it for now. Thank you for your time. I'll let you get back to your work."

Sofia stood. "Yes, thank you. I have much to get back to."

Vasily escorted her to the door. When she left the room and the double doors closed behind her, she let out a sigh of relief.

#

Back in the office, Petrovich strolled over to the fireplace and grasped the poker again. "Do you believe her?"

Vasily stood, emotionless. "No."

Nikoli stabbed at the logs, causing glowing ash to ascend like a swarm of fireflies up the chimney.

He turned back to his henchman.

"Neither do I."

6

Petrovich Research Facility
   Eastern Siberia, Russia
   December 14th
   20:20 Local Time

#

Nikoli's behavior had been eating at her all day. It wasn't normal. Something was wrong.

Why would a billionaire who allows everyone to do things for him be out in the woods slaughtering wolves? And how did he know it was my car stopped on the road? Did he check the gate logs for the time I left?

Sofia cleared her mind and reviewed her programming and usage data. As she and her team worked to correct deficiencies in the array, there was an abnormality demanding her attention.

Well, it makes little sense. According to this data, they have tested it more times than I can account for. And, at a much higher power rate. What the hell?

She tried accessing additional files when she ran into a roadblock.

Blocked? Why are these records restricted? I'll get around this. You're not keeping me out.

Her boyfriend, Colon, during her time at Cambridge, was studying software engineering and computer science. His skills went beyond standard coding and development. He was a talented and experienced hacker. His abilities fascinated her. Once while she stood by, he bypassed the school's firewalls and hacked the main server containing students' grades. Within minutes, he had changed one of his friend's scores from failing to passing.

A few quick clicks and a couple of taps on the keyboard and he was done; an easy hundred pounds for his effort. Before she left school, he'd taught her a thing or two about how to do it. Unfortunately for him, he got caught and expelled from the university. His father made him move back home and refused to pay for any more schooling. She hadn't talked to him in years.

After several unsuccessful attempts, Sofia broke into the data server and accessed the database. It took her less than fifteen minutes to gain administrative rights to her needed records. With wide eyes, she placed her hand over her agape mouth.

Oh, my God. Those weren't tests.

She scrolled and read further.

Those were full strength! What is he doing?

All those times, when the facility was supposed to be closed to employees for 'security reasons', a holiday or some other excuse. She examined one of those dates, and it brought back a memory. She launched a browser and looked for any catastrophic occurrences on a particular day when a test had been conducted. There had been. Then, after looking through the other dates, she was forced to confront her worst fears.

Holy shit! He's using the array and causing all these disasters. But why?

Sofia realized if she sent an email, Petrovich would intercept it. Then she had an idea. She brought up a Tor Browser, a second generation of *onion routing*, which she also learned from her former boyfriend.

Colon had set up an anonymous remailer for his 'clients' and she had an account on his mail server. She typed a message to Colon and fished in a secret 'pocket' in her purse for a tiny one-gigabyte flash drive which had her private PGP Key. She encrypted the email and sent it to Colon's remailer.

Even if Petrovitch intercepted it, he could never decrypt it. The encoded transmission would go to Colon's remailer, where it would get four extra layers of forwarding addresses. On each destination. The IP address would change to the next remailer in the chain until the final one would forward to Colon's email account.

Such a message would be impossible for anyone to trace the originating address. Sofia was sure he would keep his old system running as most anonymous remailers had been closed down.

He would also have her PGP Public Key. As he didn't speak Russian, she doubted if he would bother to attempt translating it. He would send it to Nestor Larkin's secure email address. She finished the note and sent it off as the door to her lab opened.

Nestor was part of a group of close friends she had at Russian New University. He was a tall, thin, quirky fellow, but he made her laugh. His dark, moppy hair only added to his clown-like personality. She had always sensed his attraction and affection for her, but she always regarded him more as a brother, nothing more. She was also aware there was nothing he wouldn't do for her, enabling her to take advantage.

Included were instructions to put the info on a flash drive and hide it in a specific location. She told him she would be there this weekend to get it and take it to the proper authorities. The door opened. She clicked send.

Vasily stepped into her office. "Why are you still working here so late?"

She closed all the screens on her monitor as he approached her desk. "Finishing up. I had some items I needed to get done today. What are you doing here? Bringing me some more tea?"

She attempted to gauge Vasily's reaction with a forced smile, but the man remained stoic with a stern expression.

"Mr. Petrovich would appreciate a moment. You can come back for your things later."

Her stomach churned with a sense of unease and the hairs on the nape of her neck stood on end.

"Oh shit! They know something. They know I accessed the files. What am I going to say? I'll play dumb."

Petrovich met them in the corridor halfway to his office. "Miss Kuzma. A pleasure to see you again so soon."

She smiled and brushed her blond hair behind her ear. "You can call me Sofia, remember?"

"But of course. I apologize." Nikoli's arm enveloped Sofia's shoulder as he guided her toward his office along the hallway.

"Sofia, you have been extremely busy and are an invaluable employee to me. I like to get to know my top people on a more personal level. After you left my office, I realized we haven't had the opportunity."

He scratched his nose and dipped his chin. His mannerisms were more like those of a pubescent boy asking for a first date than those of a confident man. "What are you doing this weekend?"

She felt the blood rush to her cheeks. "Gosh, Mr. Petrovich. I'm honored you've asked me, but I'm afraid I have to take some time off."

Nikoli stopped and swiveled around to her. "Oh? How come?"

Sofia sighed and moved her eyes away from Petrovich's gaze. "It's my mother. She's fallen ill and needs my help. I must go to Moscow and take her to several doctor's appointments and then stay with her for a while."

Nikoli's eyes narrowed, and he grasped his chin. "You omitted this at our earlier meeting."

She turned and peered along the hallway toward his office. "Yes, I know. I only got the call about an hour ago."

"This is bad news. I am sorry to hear this. What about your father?"

She pivoted back to Petrovich. "I'm afraid he passed a few years back."

He placed his hand on her shoulder and squeezed gently. "Condolences to you and your mother." He released her, and they continued to walk. "Moscow is over two-thousand miles away. How do you intend to get there?"

"I'm taking a train to Bratsk and then flying from there."

"Still, a time-consuming and tiresome journey. I will have Vasily drive you to Mirny. That part is a long trip. A woman shouldn't be out in the middle of Siberia alone. Especially in your old car. How many days do you plan on being away?"

"As little as possible. I know we have a major test coming on January 10th. As of now, we're ahead of schedule, but I'll be taking my computer with me to work on some non-essential things."

Nikoli stopped, turned, and faced her. She backed up against the wall as he came closer, his proximity overwhelming. "I was hoping you'd attend a conference with me in Tver next week. There are a lot of parties before and afterwards, and I was looking forward to getting to know you better."

"Thank you, sir, I appreciate it, but..."

Having backed Sofia against the wall, Nikoli placed his hands on either side of her head, effectively trapping her. "You know, most people would jump at the chance to go with me. Were you aware Russia has more billionaires than any other country in the world?"

A wave of nausea crept over her. Her heart raced from nervousness. "Yes sir, and you're one of them," Sofia pressed herself back as close to the wall as possible and forced a smile.

"One of them?" Nikoli scoffed. "I am *the* one. The richest man in all of Russia and soon—soon, I will be the richest man in the world."

Nikoli leaned in to her left ear, closed his eyes and inhaled. He then whispered, "Are you sure you want to pass on this opportunity?"

Sofia fought the urge to turn her head as the pungent smell of vodka assailed her nostrils. "I am so sorry, but she's my mother. If it were anyone else, I would come. I'm sorry, but I have to go. I hope you don't hold it against me."

She placed a gentle palm on his chest and smiled. "A raincheck?"

"I understand." Unhappy, Nikoli removed his left hand from the wall, allowing Sofia to leave.

Sofia flashed another smile. "I am sorry. But thank you."

Nikoli nodded. His frown displayed his disappointment. "No problem. Next time."

"Yes, for sure. Next time."

Sofia made her way toward the exit with purpose, a brisk step, but not so much as to suggest she was trying to escape. "Oh, Miss Kuzma?"

Sofia stopped and closed her eyes. She took a breath, turned around, and smiled. "Yes?"

"You're forgetting your laptop."

She turned back to face him and Vasily. "Oh, of course. My mind is all over the place. Thank you."

Sofia headed back to her office to get her computer.

When she turned the corner and her footsteps faded, Vasily leaned into Nikoli and said, "She's lying. Her mother died eight years ago."

"You fucking think I didn't know? Find out what all she accessed and who she sent it to."

"We've already tried. She used some type of encrypted method to send the email."

They continued to Nikoli's office. He pushed open both double doors with force. The bang resonated inside his office. Nikoli went straight to the bar, poured himself a vodka, and shot it back.

With the empty glass in his hand, he motioned toward Vasily. "What about the key loggers we put on everyone's machines?"

He shook his head. "She must have bypassed it. All we have is the recipient's mail address, and that is an account on an anonymous server. Anyone might be the owner and we have no way of knowing if that is the actual recipient."

Nikoli brushed his hand through his dark hair. "Dammit! Then fucking find out who it was. Send him an email. Something he'd respond to. Examine the metadata on the headers. It will give us an origin."

He poured another drink. "In the meantime, call her and get her travel schedule so you can take her to the station. Put someone on the train to follow her. Someone she won't recognize." Nikoli pointed to Vasily. "And you. You get to Moscow, or wherever the hell she's going, find this person she is meeting and take care of it."

He chugged the second drink.

Back at her residence, Sofia booked her train and flight. She would wait until she was at the airport to send her schedule to Nestor. She poured herself a glass of wine. The idea of having to ride in a car with Vasily for several hours raised her anxiety. She relaxed and contemplated her next steps.

7

London, England
 December 14th
 11:31 AM Local Time

#

A familiar sound roused Colon Fuller from his slumber, throwing him back to a not-too-distant time. He lay on his belly in a state of stupor as his wits tried to catch up with him.

Wait a minute. Did I hear what I imagined I did?

After a couple of minutes, He started dozing off, when the chime filled his ears once again.

As he pushed the blankets aside, both eyelids opened wide. Raising himself, he sat on the edge of the bed, tugging on his beard and rubbing his eyes.

No way. Not her. I haven't had contact with her in years.

Throwing back the covers, he swung his legs around and shuffled over to his home office. It comprised a desk with multiple desktops and laptops and twice as many monitors.

Sitting in his black leather gaming chair stitched with red piping, he pulled over a wireless keyboard linked to an old desktop. He took an air can and blew over the filth-covered board. Dust filled the air, and he coughed and waved his hand to dissipate the rubbish the compressed gas dislodged.

His fingers rattled the keys. He opened the admin panel, managing the backend of his onion router platform. A tool he used when he was back at Cambridge to communicate with his 'clients' when he did considerable hacking on the side.

The system notified him when somebody forwarded an email through his remailer. Since certain customers were more important than others, and he wanted to make sure their messages got through, he reprogrammed the anonymous remailer server to play a distinctive sound whenever specific people accessed his system. Although he hadn't heard that unique chime in years, he knew it belonged to a memorable individual.

The administration screen opened, and he clicked his mouse to navigate his interface.

Let's see if you are who I think you are.

His eyes widened, and his stomach felt a little queasy. He selected the queue and then the email header.

"Bloody hell. Sofia. What are you up to?"

He tried to open the communication, but it was PGP encrypted and she hadn't attached her Public Key.

Damn! It could take hours. Did I back it up somewhere? If I did, I have no idea where I put it. What was her alias name? It wasn't her surname.

He connected to one of the PGP Key servers and typed in 'Sofia'. Hundreds of entries filled the screen. Lounging in his chair, he fixed his gaze on the monitor, searching for inspiration.

Oh dammit! What was that chick's pseudonym? Something to do with her cat…

He rose and sauntered over to the kitchen. A piece of leftover chocolate cake sat alone in the fridge and some lukewarm coffee aged in the percolator, but he gulped down a few mouthfuls. The caffeine jolted him awake.

Cake! Kandy! Got it!

Colon typed 'Sofia KandyKake' and hit 'Enter'. There it was. He downloaded the key and decrypted the transmission. It had two parts.

Hi Colon, it's been a while. I hope all is okay with you, because I need your help. I may have uncovered something horrible about the man I work for. If he finds out I discovered this information, I could be in danger. I must get a message to a friend in Moscow right away, but I dare not write anything in plain text.

So, I'm sending it through the same encrypted tunnel we used in the old days. Colon, my guy doesn't know PGP, but he has a proprietary secure mail account. Will you forward the attached communication to him through a secure line? His email address is nessie@lochness.biz.

The rest of the message was in Russian. He'd finished the basic Russian course, so he translated it with a little help from his dictionary, writing the translation on a notepad.

Nestor, I hope everything is going well. There isn't much time to write this, so I'll get straight to the point. Nikoli Petrovich, the man I've been working with for several years, has built a High-frequency Active Auroral array.

It's my belief he is the one that has caused some of these natural disasters. He is responsible for the tsunami that hit Sri Lanka last year and perhaps Fukushima two years ago as well.

I have evidence that I am going to send you. Please transfer this information and copy it to a flash drive. Put it in the shiny C you gave me and keep it at the store. Do not tell anyone! Delete this after you're done. I'll be there in a couple of days to pick it up. I'll let you know when I arrive in Moscow. Thanks so much. And be careful.

Sofia

Colon sat and reread the missive several times. This knowledge was chilling. Sofia would never lie about something like this, and if it's true, we need to stop this bastard.

Colon forwarded the correspondence as she had requested and sent an encrypted copy to his work email. He dressed, grabbed a sandwich, and headed out for Thames House.

After they expelled Colon from Cambridge, he stayed out of school for a year. He continued to improve his hacking skills by playing pranks. They were simple and harmless in his eyes. Things like changing corporations' websites to display erotica instead of their normal images.

Once he hacked into the electrical signage in the West End Theater District and displayed a Photo Shopped image of someone from the Royal Family in a provocative outfit with Jeffrey Epstein in the background. They almost caught him, and if they had, he was looking at prison time. But he covered his tracks well and backed off the shenanigans permanently.

Even though they kicked him out of Cambridge, he must have left an impression. He would forever be thankful to the Dean, who had him dismissed since it propelled him to his current position.

While he was finishing his degree at the non-prestigious University of East London, he got a call from Lucy Roberts, the Director General of MI5.

It turned out Lucy was a former student of the Dean who expelled him. She sometimes reached out to him for leads on any candidates and he had given her Colon's name and number.

Colon entered the headquarters of MI5, scanned his badge, and went to his cubicle. His boss, Peter McCullen, saw him come in and went over to question him.

Peter was an old-school agency guy who'd been there for 40 years and was looking to retire in the next 2 years. There was a digital countdown clock he hung on his office wall. The sense he had for fashion was horrific. He wore a brown and gold plaid 3-piece suit and a boring blue tie.

Whenever Colon glimpsed at his smile, he couldn't help but notice how one of his front teeth stood out. It was gray and larger than its counterparts, which further fueled the stereotype of British people having poor dental hygiene.

"What are you doing here? I thought you were on the late shift for the next three weeks?"

"I am." He turned and scanned his surroundings. "But I have to speak to you."

Peter's smile waned. He waved his arm. "Come on. My office."

They entered his office. He glanced at the countdown clock.

665 days

He motioned for Colon to sit on the well-worn brown leather couch in front of his desk while Peter opted to rest against it.

Peter leaned in. "Okay. What did you want to talk to me about?"

Colon took a deep breath and closed his eyes to relax. When he exhaled, he met his boss' gaze.

"I think I stumbled onto something significant. Like, massive."

He waited for a reaction, but Peter kept cool.

"And? What is it?"

"When I was at Cambridge, I created an onion router and a mail relay service for my—customers so we could keep it encrypted and anonymous and not get caught."

Peter nodded. "Yes, I know all of this. But you got nicked, and that's how you got your job here, and—where are you going with this?"

Colon raised his hand and pointed. "Okay, I didn't get—caught."

He made air quotes. "Someone was blabbing, and a university employee overheard and started an investigation. So, it had nothing to do with my technology or hacking. I want to make that clear."

Peter closed his eyes and nodded. "Okay, fine. Get to the point."

Colon blinked. "Right. Sorry." He stood and paced in the room. "I had a ton of contacts and I devised alerts, some unique, so I would know when anyone was using the mail server relay and sending messages. A lot—"

He chuckled. "And I mean a shitload of people had access to my anonymous remailer service, so I figured—with the position I have now at MI5, I'd keep it open in case I caught an individual doing something nefarious, I could stop them—or, at least report them. Make sense so far?"

Peter stood and moved to the back of his desk. He pulled back his chair and sat. "I'm guessing you're going to tell me something similar has happened."

"Yeah, but it wasn't anyone I expected. It was my old girlfriend from when I went to Cambridge."

Peter clasped his hands, leaned forward, and rested his elbows on his desk. He listened as Colon walked about the room.

Colon continued to pace when he stopped. "Have you heard of Nikoli Petrovich?"

Peter straightened in his chair and turned to Colon. "Of course. Name someone who hasn't. What does this have to do with him?"

"Do you remember the horrible earthquake last year off the coast of India and Sri Lanka?"

"Who could forget? It killed almost a quarter million people. Not to mention the billions in pounds of damage. I think it was this Petrovich chap's disaster relief company who was first at the scene to give aid."

"Yeah." Colon wagged a finger at Peter. "That's what's so strange about this message I decrypted from Sofia. She was messaging a friend in Moscow saying she had proof this Petrovich guy caused the earthquake."

Peter scoffed. "Rubbish. How can anyone initiate a seismic event?"

"No, no, no." Colon walked to Peter's desk. "Can I use your computer?"

Peter slid the keyboard over to Colon. He rattled off some keys and visited a webpage. "She mentioned this auroral array thing he constructed, and I researched it. The Americans built one, years ago in Alaska, and for the longest time, there have been conspiracy theories around it, and one of those suppositions is it can cause earthquakes."

Peter leaned in and scanned the monitor.

Colon continued to type and displayed another webpage. "It also said it can make it rain and check out this." He pointed to the screen. "I've found several articles about this Petrovich guy claiming he's made it rain in some of these places in Africa. And he said he did it with this array."

Colon waited for Peter to finish reading. After he finished, he leaned back in his chair and glanced at the ceiling while he tapped his fingers in thought.

Peter turned to Colon. "I think we've crossed over into MI6 territory. I'll call the Director General and see what she says. In the meantime—you said she's meeting someone in Moscow?"

"Yeah, but I don't know who. Only his name is Nestor."

"No surname, no address?"

Colon shook his head. "No. Nothing. She only said she'd see him in a couple of days."

"And when did she send this message?"

Colon glanced at his watch. "Less than an hour ago."

Peter stood. "Okay, well, she's got to get there, right? You've got clearance. Check her credit card and see if she's purchased plane or train tickets anywhere. Depending on where she's coming from, we'll have a field agent from MI6 find her and follow her."

Colon nodded.

Peter lifted his phone receiver. "You get on those tasks and I'll let the Director General get with MI6 and iron out their side. We'll sort this out."

8

Train to Bratsk
  December 15th
  09:00 (01:00 GMT)

\#

Joseph Baranov handed the phone to his wife, Asami Hiraoka. "Study it, then delete it."

She studied the photograph of the young blonde woman for a few minutes and then deleted the image. She attempted to hand it back to him, but he was preoccupied. Joseph's head turned from one side to the other as he scanned the busy depot for the woman in the photo. She tapped her husband's arm with the device to attract his attention. "Here, take it. Do we know what car she'll be in?"

He took the phone and put it in his coat pocket. "No. We'll split up before we get on the train and then search for her. So far, we have only bare information. I hate it when we get pulled off an assignment to take on another without a proper briefing." He placed the tiny receiver in his right ear and fidgeted with it until it was comfortable. "Got your comm?"

Asami nodded and inserted the communicator in her left. "Okay, let's go and do this." The Baranovs were a husband-and-wife team working for the Public Security Intelligence Agency (PSIA), also known as *Kokka Anzen Hosho-bu* in Japan.

Joseph was a second generation born Russian-Japanese. His

grandparents fled Russia at the end of World War Two and moved to Japan. Joseph's father had worked for them and the apple didn't fall far from the tree. His genetics made him a perfect candidate, so he could blend into any Caucasian predominant country.

After boarding the train from the rear, the steward stopped him. "Ticket, please."

Joseph fumbled in his wallet to find it and presented it to the man, who clipped a hole in one side. He smiled. "Welcome aboard, sir." He squinted to read it, then extended his arm as a guide. "Ah, yes, you will be midway along this car on the left. Enjoy the ride."

"Thank you."

After finding his seat and placing his bag in the bin above, he plopped in the green velvet chair, offering ample cushioning, and tested out the comms with his wife.

His eyes scanned the platform out of the window, hoping to catch a glimpse of Sofia, the woman their handlers had tasked them to track. "You owe me. My seat sucks."

"First class is excellent. I'm sure I can find a way to pay you back for your sacrifice."

He chuckled. "Oh, I've already thought of several ways, and looking forward to it, my love."

The sound of a cabin door opening and closing came across the comm. Joseph shook his head and rolled his eyes. "I hope you like your private quarters."

"I do, I do."

"Fantastic. Once you're situated, connect with HQ and tell me the background of this mission."

"Yes, dear, but first I'm going to freshen up in my own personal bathroom. Give me a few minutes."

The bravado in her tone was too much. He tried to squash the ire pushing to the surface. Of course, she was teasing to get a rise out of him, and he knew it. Displaying his agitation would only encourage her, so he relented. He loved her regardless.

Asami met Joseph at the training academy twenty-six years ago. He fell in love the moment he set eyes on her. He learned quickly not to let her five-foot stature fool him. She was Yodan, or 4th-degree black belt in Aikido and Sandan, a 3rd-degree in Shito-ryu Karate and wasn't afraid of any man.

She pulled her laptop from her bag and waited for it to boot. When it was ready, she connected to the internet and downloaded her encrypted email from the agency's servers. After downloading the message, she opened her wallet and took out a tiny thumb drive. It contained files with various cooking recipes.

After inserting the USB device into her computer, she selected the file containing her private key to decrypt the message.

His earpiece chirped. "Okay, I got the background. Want to hear it?"

"Of course." He stood while scanning over the people coming onto the train. "I'm going to walk around and try to spot her as you carry on talking and updating me."

"No problem. So, to start off, she apparently works for Nikoli Petrovich. The man we suspect is behind the tsunami at Fukushima. She discovered evidence of this and sent it to an old friend in Moscow. Oh, and I know why they pulled us off our assignment at such short notice."

"How so?" He turned sideways to get by someone in the aisle.

"The agency had gained access to a known hackers' anonymous relay server in the UK a few years ago. He's been quiet for some time, and we'd assumed he'd quit and retired. Well, turns out he now works for MI5. Anyhow, our cyber squad succeeded in intercepting an encrypted communication she transmitted to him. Our team has not yet managed to copy or crack her secret key. However, the guy they sent it to, this Nestor someone, was using simple POP email software, and they got the message. The fool left it on his laptop in plain text. Most people are too dumb to operate a computer."

The door at the end slid open, and he walked to the next car. "Okay, go on."

"So, what we know is his name is Nestor, and he is in Moscow. Because we were the only agents sufficiently close to the station to catch this train, they pulled us off our other assignment to locate her and follow her. Our mission is to find out who she transmitted the information to and retrieve it by any means possible."

"Okay, sounds simple enough."

There was a long pause. Joseph carried on searching the faces of the surrounding women, trying to identify Sofia when he realized the silence. "What aren't you telling me?"

"Our friends at MI6 are also aware. We have to be prepared. They will have someone on this train."

Joseph rubbed his hands together. "Well, as far as I'm concerned, it's an extra pair of eyes. If we can spot him, he can help us find her. But—" He turned, then proceeded to the last car and stopped in the space between the cars. "We need to assume Petrovich knows everything we do. He will have people on the train as well."

Asami cleared her throat. "Mmm, right."

"You remain in the first part of the train. Miss the first class and I'll stay in the back. Let me know if you discover her and I'll buy an upgrade. Keep your comm open."

#

"Thank you. Your loyalty has not gone unnoticed."

Nikoli slammed the receiver back onto the rest. "Fuck!" He dialed Vasily.

"I don't know what the hell is going on around here, but I got off the phone with a valuable contact. There are not one, but three fucking agents on the train looking to follow Sofia and get the data she sent. One from MI6 and the other two from Japan's intelligence. I only have a picture of the MI6 agent. I'll send it to you."

He drummed his fingers on the surface of his desk. "Let whoever you have following the bitch know they'll have to figure out who the other two are. Take them all out! We cannot allow them to acquire the particulars about our system! Got it?" After the call with Vasily, Petrovich called his two top information technology gurus to his office. Both men entered the office with trepidation. Walking slowly, with their heads on a swivel, they searched the room for any of Petrovich's henchmen.

"The pair of you. Get over here. Now!" He reached for an apple from a bowl of fruit on his desk.

The two guys went to a slow jog to the front of their employers' desk. Nikoli pointed to the man on his left. "You. You're Jiri, correct?" He bit into the apple and chewed.

Jiri nodded. "Yes, Mr. Petrovich."

Nikoli motioned with his hand, holding the fruit toward the other man. "And you. You're his boss, right?"

The man also nodded. "Yes, sir, Mr. Petrovich."

"Josef, if I recall, correct?"

Josef smiled and nodded again. "Yes, sir."

Nikoli finished chewing, swallowed and threw the rest of the apple in the trash.

"Not anymore." He retrieved a pistol from his drawer and shot Josef in the head. Blood splattered on Jiri's face and he continued to stand at attention, ignoring the sweat and bits of brain matter trickling down his face.

"We've had too many leaks. You're now in charge. Make sure it never happens again."

Jiri took a deep breath and exhaled. "Yes sir, Mr. Petrovich."

"You're dismissed."

#

Vasily chose Gregori to follow Sofia. He was new and had never met or seen her in person, so there was no chance she would recognize him or suspect he was following her. With his hair pulled back in a ponytail and wearing a dark blue suit, he appeared to be like any other business executive traveling on to a conference or symposium. Although his six-foot-five-inch frame and muscular build caused him to stand out from the other passengers.

Knowing she was in first class, he purchased a ticket of equal standing and made his way to the lounge car. The bar occupied the corner on the opposite end of the carriage, leaving an open area spotted with various chairs and sofas with cocktail tables. All with a vista of the broad expanse of Siberia, outside the panoramic windows. Spotting an unoccupied seat with a clear view of the car, he settled in, taking in the man sitting across from him in gray joggers and hoodie.

#

Asami stepped out of her exclusive room and walked toward the front of the train. Stepping into the next car, she followed the path along the far side of the carriage, passing more private suites on her way. As she began to enter the next car, she met a conductor, heading in the opposite direction. As he attempted to pass her, he smiled. "Pardon me, Ma'am."

Her eyes sparkled as she beamed at him. "Oh, sir? I was wondering if you could help me."

He turned back to face her. "I'll try my best. What can I do for you?"

"I'm meeting a friend of mine for a girl's weekend. It's her birthday and I want to surprise her with a gift in her suite when she arrives. It's a card I'd like to slip under the door. Could you tell me what room she's in?"

The conductor sighed. "I'm not supposed to do this, but." He reached into his jacket pocket and withdrew an iPad mini. His fingers tapped several times on the screen. "What's her name?"

"Oh, thank you so much. I call her Sofia. Her full name is Sofia Kuzma. We attended the same school, and we haven't met up for some time."

He made a few more gestures with his hand as he navigated the screens. "She's in C7. You didn't hear it from me."

She gasped and grinned as her eyes widened. "Oh, much appreciated, sir." She placed a gentle touch on his forearm. "It was so kind of you to help."

The conductor went on his way through the carriage. When he'd turned the corner to move to the next car, Asami activated her communicator.

"Joseph."

"Yeah, you got something?"

"Yes. I found out what room she's in."

"Have you been attempting to hack into their system, too? I've been trying and can't get past their damn firewall."

Her brow furrowed. "No. I asked a conductor." Her lips curled into a smile. "He couldn't resist my charm."

"Nobody can, my dear. It's impossible."

She made her way back to her car as she spoke. "Aww, aren't you sweet?" She opened the door to the subsequent car. "You're never going to guess where she is."

"Where?"

"Right freaking next to me."

She rounded the corner to walk toward her suite when a door opened.

"Hold on a second."

A tall, attractive blonde woman emerged wearing a red cocktail dress. She turned to Asami and nodded. "Hello."

Asami returned the smile. "Hi there."

Sofia changed direction and walked toward the lounge car.

Unlocking the door to her suite, she stepped in and closed the door. "It would appear you're getting an upgrade after all. That was her. She's making her way to the lounge car."

"Roger. Does she resemble her picture? What is she wearing?"

"Oh, you won't miss her. Beautiful tall blonde in a red cocktail dress. She has a choker of pearls and a pair of beautiful earrings."

"Meh, not my type."

"Better not be." Asami reached into her purse and retrieved her pistol. "I'm going there now. When you arrive there, start a conversation and see what information you can extract from her. Don't flirt too much. I'll be watching."

Joseph laughed. "I wouldn't dare."

After upgrading his ticket, he took his luggage to his private room. It was the car before the lounge car. He changed into something more appropriate, based on what Sofia was wearing. He put on a black suit with a blue shirt, no tie, and strode in the direction of the lounge car.

#

Trevor Stone sipped his Old Fashioned, when a beautiful young woman entered and approach the barman. Her beauty was striking, and the red dress hugged her curves like an expensive sports car on a winding mountain road.

And she's, my mark. Thank you, God. I should have worn something nicer than these damn joggers.

The door on the opposite end of the car opened and a gentleman of average height wearing a black suit walked in.

From what he could tell, Sofia ordered some kind of martini. As the gentleman in the suit approached the bar, she acknowledged him with a smile, and her eyes searched around to find a seat.

The man in the black suit ordered and paid for his drink. Then, he turned back toward Sofia and eyed her while he took a sip of his cocktail.

Well, you dirty old man. I know what you're thinking. I don't blame you either. However, I need to check out who you are.

Being as clandestine as he could, Trevor took out his smartphone, leaned over as if he was reading it, and tilted it to take a photo. After a few minutes, his phone chimed, and he studied the abbreviated dossier on the Japanese operative.

Fucking fantastic. Competition.

#

Gregori sat and read *Sovetsky Sport*, a daily Russian sports publication, with his eyes peeking over the top. Satisfied the MI6 agent was sitting still to observe, he now focused on the man in black.

He must be one of the other agents Mr. Petrovich told us about.

Gregori stood and went to the bar. He acknowledged the man in black and spoke to him in Russian. "It's a hell of a view, isn't it?" He gestured toward Sofia, and both men nodded and laughed.

Joseph motioned at her with the hand holding his cocktail. "Indeed, it is. I think I'll say hello."

As he gestured, his jacket opened and Gregori spotted the butt of a pistol tucked into his pants. Gregori focused on the man's ear. There was a tiny pull pin on the communicator sticking out of the ear canal. "Best of luck."

He paid for a club soda with lime. Once the bartender handed him his drink, he returned to his seat to observe. The man in black sauntered over to Sofia and asked if he could sit in the unoccupied seat. There were now two of the three people Petrovich instructed him to eliminate in the carriage with him. His gaze stared past Sofia and the gentleman in black as he tried to eavesdrop on their conversation.

After what seemed like an eternity of meaningless banter and small talk, the man in black said something, piquing his interest.

"I have something I think you'll be interested in. It's in my quarters in the next car. I'll retrieve it."

Gregori buried his face in the sports section and waited as his mark walked by and exited the car. He let a few seconds pass before folding the paper, standing, and leaving the car.

In between the cars, the clackety-clack of the train's wheels rolling along the rail reverberated in this space. It would help to muffle any sound. Continuing to focus on the next car, looking out for his target, he took a moment to unlock the train's exit door.

A quick peek through the window into the next car revealed the gentleman vacating his quarters. Gregori entered the restroom, withdrew an eight-inch stiletto, and listened for the door to the next car to open. He thought through the moves he would make to take out his mark as fast as possible. The butt of the pistol in his marks' pants flowed through his mind.

A stone-cold professional killer, Gregori gripped the dagger with the tip pointing up. His hands were still, and his heartbeat held steady. Not an ounce of anxiety swept through him.

The train car door opened and Gregori exited the bathroom. He clutched the dagger by his side to hide it from his prey.

He slid to the right to let Joseph pass. "Pardon me."

His victim nodded. "No problem."

In one swift move, Gregori raised his left arm, pressed it to Joseph's neck, and used it to push him against the bathroom door. Joseph's back slammed into it with a thud. Before he could react, Gregori thrust the blade through the bottom of Joseph's jaw and pierced his brain.

Pinching the wire, he withdrew the communicator out of Joseph's ear. "I'm going to use this to draw out your wife and kill her." He laughed out loud.

He let the corpse fall to the floor. Reaching over, he opened the door. The clacking of the wheels echoed throughout the cramped space. Trees, rocks and brush flew past as the train barreled along the tracks. The wind flapping his jacket, Gregori removed Joseph's pistol and tucked it into his waistband. He stepped over the body, then heaved and rolled it down the steps and out the door.

Wiping his hands as if nothing had happened, Gregori peered through the windows of both cars to make sure the commotion had alerted no one. Seeing the Japanese woman with her eyes buried in a magazine, he proceeded back to Joseph's cabin to search for any intel. He needed to discover what they had gathered about Sofia and who, if anyone, they sent it to.

#

Immersed in the article she'd been reading, Asami hadn't been keeping track of the time. She glanced at her watch.

Where the hell is Joseph? He's been gone for 20 minutes.

She stood and turned to head back to her suite when she activated her comm.

"Hey, what's going on? You've been gone for twenty minutes."

After a few steps toward her suite and not getting a reply, the back of her neck tingled. Something was wrong.

"Joseph. Answer me."

A voice she didn't recognize interrupted the creaking of her suite door opening.

"He won't be answering you anymore."

The virtual punch in the gut hit harder than she thought. She was nauseous and stumbled into her room.

"Who is this? What did you do with him?"

In a deep, ominous tone filled with a thick Russian accent, the voice goaded her on with mysterious intent. "Come and find out."

She latched on to her Sig Sauer and pulled it from her purse.

"You're the thick oaf with the ponytail, aren't you?"

The same voice chuckled and tempted her with an ominous allure. One impossible to resist. "Come and find out."

She chambered a round, then ripped a towel off the rack to conceal the pistol. She walked out of her room and headed back to the lounge car. As she marched through the car, the MI6 agent was still sitting in his chair.

Does the fucker even know what's going on?

She breezed past him, aware of his gaze following her every move. Without breaking her stride, she pushed the button to open the door and entered the space between the cars. A pool of blood near the restroom door caught her eye.

Her heart sank as she traced it to the steps leading to the train's exit door.

Oh, my love. No.

Her heart filled with a potent mixture of hatred and unbridled anger. From that moment on, avenging her beloved husband's death became her sole and unwavering mission.

Leaving the noise of the clanking wheels behind her, she entered the next private suite car and followed the hall to the right side of the train. Each step placed with caution and silence, she readied herself for her unseen adversary.

The thumping of each heartbeat reverberated in her ears, as if counting the seconds of her fleeting existence. Every breath shuddered with a reminder of her own vulnerability, both fearful and captivated by what lay ahead.

The door on her left opened. Faster than she could react, a thick, meaty hand chopped against her arm. She lost her grip on the pistol and someone pulled her into the room.

Gregori grabbed her by the lapels and slammed her against the ceiling of the car. Without hesitation, Asami cupped her hands and slapped each on the side of Gregori's head, around his ears. Before he dropped her, she jabbed all four fingers in the middle of his throat.

Gregori bent over. His face, a reflection of the discomfort she caused. Asami raised her knee fast and delivered a blow to his forehead. As the force of the drive made him rise, she kicked him in the groin as hard as she could and turned for the door to get her pistol.

Gregori, enraged, grabbed her by the back of the collar and pulled. He slammed her body against the opposite side of the car. As he approached her, she grabbed a full bottle of vodka and broke it over the side of his head. The steel tray found its way into her hands. She swung and smashed it against his face, breaking his nose.

The beefy hunk of a man was slightly affected, but the ire within him reached a boiling point. As he came back to her, Asami kicked at him. He grabbed her leg and slammed her against the floor and then again against the opposite wall. She landed on the padded bench. Her ninety-four-pound was a mere rag doll to a man who could bench press over 650 pounds.

Asami tried to breathe. Each attempt returned a sharp pain.

Shit. He broke a couple of my ribs.

An image of Joseph flowed through her mind's eye. She remembered the two *kanzashi* in her hair.

How could I have been so stupid?

She placed her hands back over her head.

"Fuck you, you dumb Russian. Are you going to kill me too, like you did my husband?"

Gregori stood, wiped the blood off his face with his sleeve, and spat. He chuckled.

"Yes, but I think I will have my way with you first."

The oversized oaf unfastened his pants and bent over her. In one move, she grabbed the *kanzachi* from her hair and drove them deep into Gregori's clavicles. He screamed in pain.

The Russian's temper blew through the roof. He grabbed her and threw her against the door. Not wasting a second, he lifted her over his head and threw her toward the window, shattering it and sending glass and Asami out onto the tracks.

#

Gregori spent the next hour fixing his injuries before he returned to the lounge car. When he entered, Sofia was engaged in conversation with an older couple, and the man in sweats he identified as the MI6 agent was no longer there. He stepped over to the bar.

"Vodka. Straight."

He slammed back the drink, placed the glass on the bar, and nodded for another.

"The man in the tracksuit—the sweats. Where did he go?"

The bartender shook his head. "I don't know. I only took over from the other guy a few minutes ago, but I didn't see anyone wearing sweats when I came in."

Gregori drank the vodka and asked for a third. He took it to his old seat, grabbed the sports paper, and waited.

9

Train to Bratsk
    December 15th
    17:20 (11:20 GMT)

#

Trevor waited a moment before deciding to leave and plant his tracker. Sofia was engaged in a lengthy conversation, and the other suspected Japanese agents appeared to be occupied. He tossed back the rest of his cocktail, stood, and sauntered over to the bar, where he placed his empty glass. He waved to the bartender and mouthed 'thanks'.

The clacking of the wheels filled his ears as he left the lounge car. Trevor checked behind him to make sure he wasn't being followed. He reached into his pocket to retrieve one of his favorite tools.

The electric lock pick made quick business of the trains' antiquated and poor door locks. Upon entering her room, the delicate, lingering fragrance of a floral perfume greeted him. Its sweet and airy notes intertwined with each other, filling his senses with a soft and feminine charm.

It was easy to understand the effect Sofia's beauty could have on a man. He carefully rummaged through her belongings, not wanting to disturb anything, until he found her laptop case resting on the bench.

Perfect.

He hid a small, round gadget in an unused internal zipper pocket. It was a quarter the size of an air tag, but five times stronger. Before opening the door, he listened for any approaching footsteps. When he was comfortable nobody was coming, he stepped out of Sofia's room and went to his own, just two down. Once inside, he opened an app on his smartphone and activated the device.

This is going to be simple.

#

Bratsk Train Station
December 16th
10:00 (02:00 GMT)

Trevor felt refreshed after a few hours of sleep. He sat in the dining car and sipped his coffee while he scanned over the crowd of people disembarking from the train. With a quick peek at his phone, the flashing icon showed Sofia was on the move. Knowing they were on the same flight to Moscow, he was in no hurry, so he finished his coffee.

Through the mass of scattering people, he could see some travelers moving out of the way of several policemen drawing near the train. His defense tactics kicked in, and he began to think of his next action.

There's no reason they'd be coming for me. It must be something else.

He saw three officers stop and talk to the conductor. The guy motioned and pointed toward the adjacent car, then continued his conversation. Curiosity getting the best of him, he grabbed his bag and coat. As he stepped off, he turned to glance over his shoulder. There was a broken window, and under it were dried blood trails flowing in the direction of the back of the carriage.

#

Vasily stood outside the train station and threw his cigarette on the ground. During the time he was in the air on Petrovich's private jet, he received a call from Nikoli. They'd intercepted some of Sofia's calls to Nestor while she was on the train and had pieced enough information together to figure out who he was. Vasily waited for the broad depot sign to show the train had arrived before calling Gregori.

"Da."

"Plans have changed. Did you take care of the problems we had on the train?"

Gregori stepped off the train and kept his eye out for the British agent. "No. I got the two from Japan, but the other eluded me. He was wearing a gray running suit with a hoodie and trainers."

He paused for effect. "After I handled the woman, I returned to where he had been sitting, observing Miss Kuzma, but he was no longer there, and I didn't see him for the rest of the trip. He must have changed clothes."

Vasily lit another cigarette. "Well, find him. We know who Nestor is, and now you're flying to Moscow with me. But we need to take care of this problem first."

By the time Vasily tossed away his cigarette, Gregori had sighted the MI6 agent. Vasily answered his phone. "Did you spot him?"

"He's heading toward the C door exit. Black slacks, white shirt, mid-thirties, dark brown hair. I have a syringe full of fentanyl."

Vasily picked up his pace and headed in their direction. "Have you located a place where we can intercept him?"

"Yes, I see a maintenance corridor coming up on my right. Are you close enough to help yet? It will be just after the restrooms placard hanging from the ceiling from your vantage point."

Seeing the sign, Vasily started scanning the area for their mark. "Yes, I see the sign and I see him. Five seconds."

Vasily moved toward the agent and sidestepped in front of him. They bumped into each other. Vasily smiled and dipped his chin. "Oh, apologies. My fault."

He placed his hand on Trevor's shoulder. Gregori came from behind and injected the lethal dose into his neck. Both men grabbed hold and guided Trevor toward the back of the corridor. They found an unlocked closet, dumped him on the floor, and left him to die.

In the car, Vasily dialed Petrovich and put him on speaker. "We've eliminated all three agents, boss, and we're now headed to the airport to get to Moscow."

"About damn time something went our way. What's your plan when you get to Moscow?"

"You discovered where this guy works. We're going to follow him home and get the data from him there."

"Okay, you know what to do after you get it, right? No traces."

Vasily turned to Gregori, and both men smiled and nodded. "Oh yes, we know what to do."

#

The door to the maintenance closet opened. A hand felt a slight pulse in the neck of Trevor Stone. They injected Naloxone to reverse the effects of the strong opioid and waited. After ten minutes, Trevor awoke. "What, where am I? What happened?"

The soothing voice calmed him. "You were given a lethal dose of fentanyl. I gave you a shot of naloxone to counter the drug. Had I not been watching; you would have died."

Trevor sat on the floor and propped himself against the wall. He shook his head and rubbed his eyes. "Watching?" He focused on the person who saved him. "I, I recognize you."

"You probably have a dossier on me, like I have on you. Okay, we don't have much time. I'm after Petrovich, just like you are. You're in no shape to travel, so if you've got any intel you'd like to share, our agency would be grateful, and we'd owe you a favor."

Trevor sighed. "Here. Take my phone. I put a tracker in her laptop bag. There is an app that's open and it will lead you to where she is."

"Thanks. Sit tight. I'll call an ambulance for you."

10

Moscow, Russia
December 16th
14:45 Local Time

#

Nestor Laskin darted into his flat, slammed and double-locked his door. Whether he was being followed was a mystery to him, but the sheer excitement of the possibility brought a spark to his otherwise dull life.

While on break at the Starbucks Coffee, he managed in a Northwest part of Moscow; he received an email from Sofia asking him for a favor. As usual, he happily complied. After downloading the data, he copied it to a flash drive, and hid it where she told him. Despite the madness of it all, he would do anything for the love of his life.

He removed the coat from his tall, gaunt frame and placed it over the back of a chair in his living room. He discarded his hat on the cheap, flimsy coffee table, revealing his balding head. His thoughts turned to Sofia as he imagined being her hero and how she would repay him.

Perhaps she'll come here and the bad guys will follow her. I'll kick their ass and afterwards, she'll seduce me as a thank you.

He proceeded to the kitchen and grabbed a knife from a drawer, returning to stand in front of a mirror. As he reflected upon himself, he gazed at the picture of them on the wall, taken when they were in college together, and an idea ran through his brain. He focused on his reflection and acted out his fantasy.

"Yeah, well, if you want her, you'll have to go through me. Slash, whack, punch! *Ugh!. No! We're sorry, don't hurt us.*"

"Not sorry enough! Wham, wham!"

He laughed out loud at his own silliness and admired her beauty in the photo once more. The fond memories he had of Sofia when they met in college, he would always cherish. They had a fine circle of friends. Although his hairline had faded, his desire and lust for her never did.

The painful parts of the conversation were when she spoke of her boyfriend, Colon. She would go on and on about how smart he was. Colon did this and Colon can do the other. He hated the man and was thrilled when Sofia told him he'd been expelled.

Glancing back at the mirror, he once more indulged in whimsical thoughts of protecting her from the imaginary bad guys. "Oh, you want some more, huh?" Nestor made more stabbing motions and sound effects, imagining himself saving his princess.

He paused his playful fantasy and stepped over to the photo tacked to the wall. His heart pounded and knots formed in his stomach, knowing he'd be seeing her in a few hours. He continued his theatrics in a high-pitched voice, "Oh, Nestor, you saved me. I love you."

He chuckled at his own stupidity.

A loud rapping on the door interrupted his role-playing. He placed the knife on the coffee table and went to the door. A quick peek through the peephole revealed the outline of two individuals.

"Who is it?" His voice echoed back from the door.

"Property management. We have some policy changes you need to read and sign. This will only take a minute."

Nestor reversed the deadbolt and released the chain lock. He opened the door. Two burly men stood before him: one bald and the other with a ponytail.

Vasily did the talking. "Are you Nestor Laskin?"

"Yes, what—"

He shoved him inside. Ponytail followed and slammed the door.

"Hey, what the hell? You can't barge in here and—"

A beefy hand slapped Nestor across the face. "Shut up!" He fell backward. Regaining his composure, he rubbed the red area on his face with his hand.

Vasily stepped toward him. "Where is it?"

"Where's what? You said this was—"

He lifted his arm to strike again. Nestor lifted both of his. "Wait!" Vasily held his fist cocked, ready to deliver another blow if necessary.

Nestor raised his skinny limbs. "Can you please tell me what you want, because I don't know?"

He kept focusing on the massive bald man as he reached into his jacket pocket.

Is he reaching for a gun?

He gasped. "No!"

Vasily's ham-sized fist was holding something. Nestor peered at it. "What's that?"

He shoved the object in his hand into Nestor's face. "Don't play stupid with me. It's a fucking flash drive, you moron. Now, where's the one loaded with the data Sofia Kuzma sent you?"

Nestor sighed when he saw it.

She is deep in the shit. What did she do?

Sofia's scrawny friend and wannabe savior stood and puffed out his chest with arrogant confidence. "She didn't send me anything. I've seen nothing like it in my life before. I haven't spoken to her in months. So, you can get the fuck out of here or I'm calling the police."

Nestor reached into his pocket and retrieved his phone. Vasily and Gregori turned to each other and then back to the obstinate little man. Vasily grabbed Nestor's phone and shattered it against the wall. He grasped his collar, punched him in the gut, and knocked the wind out of him. His eyes were wide with the shock of the punch. He gasped for air. Vasily pushed him back to the ground. The two goons watched as the poor man struggled for air, desperate for a breath.

Gregori clutched him by the shirt collar, lifted him from the floor, and drove his fist into his face. The impact knocked him back so hard he flipped over an easy chair and toppled a standing lamp. Vasily stomped over to him and pinched the lobe of his ear, digging his nails into it.

Nestor protested. "Stop! Please."

The bald goon released his earlobe and pointed a thick finger in his face. "You think it hurt? If you don't produce the drive in the next ten seconds, you'll find out what pain is."

Nestor grabbed a book from the floor and stood. "Screw you, assholes." He hurled the volume. It took a harmless bounce off Vasily's chest. Gregori charged in. He banged his fist hard into Nestor's stomach.

Bent over, he was reeling in torment. The agony radiated through his entire frame. A boot smashed into his ribs. He was coughing when he felt his body being lifted.

Gregori grasped hold, raised him over his head, and threw him across the room. He slammed into a table and shattered his aquarium. Water and fish spilled out onto the floor and a piece of broken glass slashed his arm. Blood gushed out, soaking his shirt and pants. Nestor focused on his wound. His mouth was agape. "Oh, my God! I'm cut bad. I need help!"

Vasily pointed at him. "Tell us what we demand."

"It's on my laptop."

"Get the computer. Now!" Vasily kicked him in his already abused ribs.

He winced in pain. When he opened his eyes, he scanned the room and spotted the knife on the table next to another photo of Sofia. "Okay. Let me get a cloth to stop the bleeding, and after I'll take you to where it is."

"No. You show us now! Later you get a towel."

Nestor was breathing hard. He squeezed his eyes tight, fighting the sensation of going into shock. "All right, it's over here."

The pathetic fool struggled to his feet and limped toward the counter while he grasped his arm. He focused on the portrait of Sofia.

I love you, Sofia. I hope you know that.

When he got to the table, he grabbed the knife, spun around, and started slashing at them.

"You sons of bitches! You'll never get it, and you'll never get her either. I'm going to kill you!" He lunged at Vasily.

Vasily batted him away as if he were a child. "Last chance, Nestor. If you don't tell us, we're going to hurt her." Vasily turned to Gregori, and the pair laughed.

Gregori had a wry smile cross his face. "But I think we'll have our way with her first. She does have an amazing ass."

Both guys burst out laughing again. Enraged, Nestor had never felt such anger and hate. It flowed through him like a fiery current, scorching every inch of his being. He gripped the knife tighter and raised it over his head. He swiveled on his heels and charged at the man with the ponytail. "No! I will kill you all!"

Vasily pulled his silenced pistol and put a slug through the side of

Nestor's head. His lifeless body landed on the floor with a thud. The two men ripped apart Nestor's apartment, looking for the flash drive.

After tearing through everything, Gregori walked into the kitchen where his partner in crime was sitting at the table.

"I tore his bedroom to pieces. I found nothing." He stared around the kitchen. All the cabinet doors and drawers were open. Vasily had dumped boxes of cereal, bottles of herbs and spices out on the counter and ground. "I'm guessing you didn't find anything either?"

Vasily had his face buried in his phone. "No." He stood. "Come on. Her plane landed. She'll be here soon. We'll wait for her in the car."

11

Moscow, Russia
    December, 16th
    17:00 Local Time

\#

As the plane touched down, Sofia powered on her phone and checked her email. The notification popped up on her screen and played a soft chime. It was from Nestor. She sensed his excitement at seeing her. He mentioned 'The Eagle Has Landed' and she giggled at his attempt to be clandestine. He confirmed where the flash card was at, but wanted her to come by his apartment so he could show her his new aquarium.

As she waited in line for a taxi, she reminisced about some of the fun times with him and her other friends. Everyone else in the group finished their studies and had moved on to have prosperous careers. All except Nestor. He was only a shift manager at a local Starbucks. There was nothing wrong with his lowly position, but she always wondered why he didn't excel at his full potential.

The cab stopped in front of an underwhelming structure. It was a 10-story concrete building, about as bland as Nestor's life. After she paid the fare, the driver went to the trunk, retrieved her suitcase, and set it on the sidewalk.

Sofia stepped out of the taxi. The cold seeped into her bones. As the sun bid farewell on the western horizon and the temperature dropped to a bone-chilling minus-five degrees Celsius, the air settled into an icy stillness. Slinging her laptop over her shoulder, she wrapped the dark wool coat around herself, grabbed her bag, and ascended the steps into the building.

She reached the third floor, and the exercise helped to warm her up. Residents decorated the halls with various Christmas decorations. Some doorways were fancier than others, but she appreciated all of them as she walked along the hall to Nestor's door. Arriving at his door, she paused prior to knocking.

Although they communicated over Facebook and emails, it had been two years since she visited him. She retained her feelings for him, but they weren't as strong as the ones she knew he had for her.

Despite leading a miserable existence, he was always happy to hear from her. She knocked and waited, anticipating an immediate response. When there was no answer, she tried again, this time louder than before.

Leaning in toward the door, she called out. "Nestor? It's me, Sofia."

One last knock, but harder. "Hey, are you ok?"

The voice inside her said something was wrong. She reached and turned the knob. It opened, so she poked her head into his apartment. "Nestor?"

Oh, shit!

The rug was littered with wet broken glass and five fish all appeared to be dead. Entering his flat, she concentrated on the area of the shattered aquarium. Upon seeing the mess, she searched for a towel to clean it up. When she turned around, her friend's lifeless corpse was lying on the ground in a pool of blood.

She placed her gloved hand over her mouth to silence her scream. Stepping toward him with caution, a numbness crept from her gut. Her whole body trembled as she wiped the tears trickling over her cheeks. In the position he was laying, she couldn't see his face. As she got closer, the single bullet hole in the side of his head came into view, as did the bone and brains. She knelt down, stroked his bald head, and sobbed.

"Oh Nestor, I'm so sorry. What have I done?" As she glanced toward the table, her picture stood in the center. The sound of two car doors closing jostled her back to the present.

Rushing to the nearest window, she peered out into the street. Three stories below, Vasily and another man with a ponytail walked to the front of the building. She spun around. Her chest was tight, and every breath intensified the vertigo.

The other man was on the train. He followed me. I have to get out of here!

She searched for Nestor's computer but didn't find it. Someone had torn the place apart.

His laptop bag was on the chair. She rushed over to it. It was empty.

Someone's taken it! Vasily!

After grabbing her bags, she ran out to the staircase, heading for the ground floor. Halfway, she met the two of them. Sophia stopped in her tracks. Vasily and she locked eyes in a tense and silent standoff. The two henchmen chased after her, their feet stomping hard as they climbed the stairs. She turned and raced back to the safety of Nestor's apartment.

The lead henchman jerked his thumb downward. "Go back and cover the exit." Gregori obeyed while he continued his pursuit.

Sofia reached the flat. Slamming the door, she secured and bolted it, scanning the room for something to block the door. She moved a chair and leaned it under the doorknob. The makeshift brace was insignificant and hardly strong enough to stop a man like Vasily, or anyone wanting in, but it would buy her some time.

Adrenaline flowed, and she perused the room for anything to use as a weapon. She spotted the knife on the floor and went to grab it, but it was covered in blood. The door splintered from the weight of Vasily as he slammed against it.

The fire escape!

She ran into the tiny kitchen and tried the window to the balcony. It was stuck. The thud of Vasily's body as he rammed his shoulder into the door got louder. She rushed to the stove and grabbed an iron skillet.

Back over to the window, turning to protect her face from any flying splinters; she swung it and smashed the glass. Using the pan, she cleared the remaining rough edges out of the way. She put one leg out onto the metal ledge and then stopped.

Shit! I need his keys!

She raced back in. The sound of the splintering door frame renewed her motivation to move faster.

Dammit! Where the hell would he keep them?

Nestor's coat hung on the back of a chair in the living room; Sofia checked his left pocket. It was empty. Wood cracked and splintered. She turned as a beefy arm came through the door.

Dashing back to the kitchen, she grabbed the iron skillet. Raising it above her head, she ran to the disintegrating door. Vasily was feeling for the lock. She swung hard and slammed the pan at his hand. He screamed and retracted his arm.

"You fucking bitch!"

Vasily peeked through the hole in the door and spotted her. Seeing his narrowed eyes and gritted teeth caused her skin to crawl. His booming voice filled the tiny flat. "What did you do with the data?"

Throwing the pan against the door, he retreated. The force left an impression on the door and the skillet clanked as it landed on the floor.

Come on! Dammit! Where the fuck are they?

She checked the other pocket and found the keys to his scooter. She pocketed them and dashed back to the kitchen and crawled out onto the platform.

Shit!

She climbed back in and grabbed her laptop, and hustled out to the top of the fire escape.

The door busting open reverberated throughout Nestor's flat.

She descended the stairs, skipping steps, like a game of vertical hopscotch.

Halfway down, she observed Vasily as he struggled out onto the landing. He winced as he fought to get his enormous frame through the opening.

Sofia continued her descent. She reached the bottom platform. An iron bracket secured the sliding ladder in its up position, blocking any access to the street below. She pressed the release lever, but it refused to budge, stuck in place with age.

Vasily was on the fire escape and closing in. The metal structure shook with every step he took. The man with the ponytail came out the front of the building. He ran toward the bottom of the fire escape. Sofia stood and stomped on the rusted lever.

"Release, dammit!"

She kicked it again. Her pursuer was getting closer.

She slammed her heel against it with each plea.

"Let!"

"Go!"

"You!"

"Asshole!"

Vasily was three meters away.

The bracket gave way. The spring-loaded ladder disengaged and slid in the direction of her pathway to freedom. It came to an abrupt halt six feet above the pavement.

In desperation, Sofia descended the ladder. At the last rung, the man with the ponytail was only a meter away. She lowered herself and hung from the bottom foot hold and swung her feet out. She connected with his chest and kicked him back and to the ground.

When he fell backward, Sofia let go of her grip and dropped to the sidewalk. Turning away, she escaped in the opposite direction and around the corner. Ahead of her, near the far side of the block, was the exit to the building's underground parking garage. She ran on the icy pavement.

Each breath caused a sharp pain in her lungs as she pushed herself to the limit. Vasily and his sidekick turned the corner in time to see her enter into the darkness. They dashed to the door and entered with weapons drawn. It was cold and dark, save for a few glowing ceiling lights. The air was heavy with the smell of exhaust fumes and oil.

Sofia was on the opposite wall, squatted at the back of a blue Volga. Kneeling on the floor, she peered under the vehicle to glimpse at the two men's shoes. Their voices resonated throughout the garage, but she couldn't make out what they were saying.

The two men split to go in opposing directions. Nervous and scared, she didn't notice she was shivering from the cold. She got to her feet from crouching behind the old Russian car, and peeked out over the hood. Neither man was in sight. Sitting across the parking area, near the exit, was a bank of scooters and bicycles. It was unclear to her which one of them belonged to Nestor.

Sofia stood and glanced both ways. Feeling confident they couldn't see her, she made her way to the scooters. The first one she tried the key wouldn't go in the hole. On to the second one, a newish Vespa didn't even have a keyhole. It used one of the new-fangled radio frequency keys.

As the sound of fast-approaching feet drew nearer, her anxiety increased. There were at least ten more for her to try. Examining the key closer, she recognized the symbol for a Tula brand of scooter. Of the remaining ones, there were only three Tulas.

As she moved toward the first one, she collided with the back of a bicycle tire, causing the bike to flip over with a thunderous crash.

The booming voice cut through her concrete prison with ease.

"Vasily, get close to the exit!"

As the footsteps approached, her anxiety increased to a level she had never experienced before. Her adrenaline peaked. The key didn't work in the first Tula she tried.

Vasily was shuffling toward her. "Sofia! Stop! We only want to talk!"

She moved to the next one. The key went into the slot. It wouldn't turn. Both pursuers closed in.

The key lodged in the keyhole as she attempted to remove it.

"Sofia! Wait!"

Struggling, she kept focusing her attention on the key, then the men, and then back to the key. Panic set in, as did the tears. "Come on, God dammit!" Pulling hard while she wiggled it, then the thing came out.

Rushing to the last scooter, she inserted it and the slot accepted it. She turned it on and hit the start button. The engine cranked but didn't start. The men were less than thirty meters away. She tried again. The engine struggled to come to life.

Come on, God dammit! Why is this happening to me?

With both goons only meters away, the engine sputtered to life. Sofia gunned the throttle and pulled the scooter out. Vasily reached out with his long arms. She could feel his hand slide off her shoulder as she went forward.

Although lowered, she still maneuvered around the barricade with enough room to spare. As she darted out onto the street, a stray bullet hit the barrier arm, sending splinters flying. Tires screeched, and a horn blared as she sped off.

Sofia had no clue where to go. Getting as far away from them as possible was her only option right now. She wouldn't endanger any more of her old friends. One dead friend was sufficient. She drove along Trerskaya, in the Tverskoy district of north central Moscow. The freezing wind rushing by made her ears red and ache. She considered reaching out to the Russian Government. After recalling the number of dignitaries and politicians Petrovich associated with, she abandoned the idea.

She could hardly trust anyone. With his billions, it was likely that he had the majority of them in his pockets. Ahead on the left was a shopping district. She spotted an entrance to an underground parking garage where she could lose her tail.

Sofia approached the entrance and came to a stop in the turning lane to let the approaching cars pass. Before she could go, a car pulled alongside her on her right. She glanced over her shoulder. Vasily sat with his firearm pointed at her.

She twisted the throttle and crossed one lane of traffic and cut off a truck. The sound of its horn blaring and the crunch of metal echoed off the tall buildings as Vasily and his partner battered their way through the bustle of vehicles to catch up.

The roar of the Mercedes' engine close behind her filled her ears. She peeked in her mirror. They were almost on her rear wheel. She spotted an opening to her right and cut through onto the sidewalk.

She waved her arm, screaming at the pedestrians. "Get out of the way!"

Blindly feeling for the horn button, she pressed it with reckless abandon.

People with bags full of Christmas presents dodged out of her way and yelled obscenities back at her. She turned north on the next street.

The two men continued to follow in pursuit. The traffic was heavy, but she maneuvered around the cars with expert precision. Vasily leaned out the window and fired his silenced pistol toward her.

Sofia passed a Fiat on its left. Its window exploding from an errant bullet. The driver sideswiped a parked car on the right.

Shit!

A sign, plastered on a building ahead, read *American Embassy*. There was an arrow at the bottom showing it was around the next corner. Sofia maneuvered around a BMW, defying the traffic laws as she swerved onto the sidewalk once again. As she navigated the turn, a patch of ice caused the rear wheel to slide out from under her. The scooter slid off the sidewalk and out onto the street. Sofia rolled along the edge of the road. A commuter screeched to a stop, but not before it slammed into her means of escape.

The Mercedes tires screeched as it came into view and hit the other car head-on, crushing the scooter between them. The crash alerted the guards in front of the Embassy a few hundred feet away. Three armed U.S. servicemen turned in her direction.

Sofia glanced at the destroyed Tula and then back to Vasily, who was taking aim. She ducked in anticipation of his happy trigger finger. The bullet struck the building behind her and ricocheted into a parked

Toyota on the street. A woman screamed as the window on the parked vehicle shattered.

She ran toward the three U.S. soldiers. "Help! Help me!"

The men spotted her running toward them. Following protocol, they all raised and aimed their rifles. "Stop! Stop now!"

Sofia continued to run in their direction. "Please! Don't shoot! Please! Those men are trying to kill me!"

She pointed at the Mercedes. The other man was inspecting the damage to his car. Vasily watched her from along the street. The Mercedes reversed from the accident and accelerated in the opposite direction. The other man waved his arms and yelled expletives, demanding they stop.

A U.S. soldier stepped forward. "On the ground! Now!"

She started to weep. "Please. They killed my friend, and they tried to shoot me."

She dropped to her knees and put her hands over her face.

"I'm sorry, ma'am, but it's out of our jurisdiction. You'll have to call the local police."

She lowered her arms and turned to the guard, who spoke to her. "No. But you don't know why they were trying to kill me. I have information. Information your government would want to hear. I don't trust ours. They're compromised. I have to talk to someone I can trust. Please! Listen to me!"

Sofia pleaded as the three soldiers all glanced back and forth at each other.

"I can tell you think I'm crazy." She continued to weep. "I'm not some whack job. I've got a doctor's degree from Cambridge. Let me speak to the person in charge. You'll be glad you did." She continued to weep and plead her case.

The men relented. One soldier helped her to her feet. They brought Sofia into the embassy and put her in an empty room, save for a metal table bolted to the floor and two chairs. There was a steel loop in the middle of the table in front of where she sat. They used it to handcuff any hostile individuals they needed to interrogate. Sofia was glad she wasn't one of them. Another embassy employee brought her a cup of hot tea with one sugar. Just how she liked it.

She'd been done with her drink for over forty minutes. She glanced at her watch when the door opened and a gentleman in a dark suit walked in.

He tossed a dossier on the table, turned the chair around so the back was facing her, and sat down. He lifted the dossier, opened it, and began reading aloud.

"Miss Sofia Kuzma. You're twenty-nine years old—doctors' degree in meteorology from Cambridge. You've been working for Nikoli Petrovich for the past two and a half years at his research facility in bum-fuck Siberia. And last but not least, you claim these two men killed your friend, uh…" He flipped through a few papers.

"Nestor Laskin. Yes. Nestor Laskin."

He closed the folder and tossed it to land near her. "So far, everything you've told us checks out. The police are at your friend's flat now."

Sofia cleared her throat and muttered. "I'm sorry. Who are you?"

"My name is Marshal Reed and I'm with the Central Intelligence Agency. I am the Chief of Station for the Moscow office. The three men you spoke to outside the Embassy said you had some information we would be interested in."

He leaned toward her. "Now—what have you got?"

12

#

Nikoli sat reading the latest information on his Active Auroral Array. He was trying to contain the rage engulfing him. The news of Sofia getting away and his men killing Nestor before finding out where he hid the data was inexcusable.

The final straw was when they informed him she was in U.S. custody and being protected. When Vasily and his companion walked into his office, he slammed his fist on his desk as he stood. Pressure rushed to his head, turning his cheeks a bright crimson. "What the hell went wrong? You told me you had her!"

Vasily held out his arms. "She got away. There was nothing we could do."

A muscle in his jaw twitched, and he pounded his fist on the table. "I know she escaped, you fucking idiot!" He pointed at his number one henchman, leaned forward, and shook an accusatory finger. "You knew where she was going to be! You had her in your sights. Why didn't you grab her?"

Nikoli banged his hand on his desk. "How did you screw this up?" Deep in thought, he paced back and forth. Then he raised a finger to his lead man. "And you killed her contact *before* you found where the data was. What were you thinking?"

The massive thug shrugged and kept quiet. Nikoli shook his head and narrowed his eyes in a stare of sheer incredulity. "Jesus, how stupid can you get? And Sofia! She was in his apartment! How did she get out?"

Vasily shifted his weight. "She climbed out of the fire escape and stole a scooter. By the time we caught her, she was in front of the U.S. Embassy. There were U.S. Soldiers. We would have been taken into custody, and—"

"I don't give a shit! It would have happened outside the embassy grounds. Out of their jurisdiction. They couldn't do anything to you!"

Vasily's eyes veered to the side. "But I thought—"

"There! There's your problem. Stop it! You do not fucking get paid to think! I pay you to do what I *tell* you to do! At the absolute worst, the police would have come and arrested you."

Nikoli pointed to himself. "Do you not remember who I am? I have connections. They would have released you and you'd be back here in less than a day. What do you believe is better? Her dead and you inconvenienced for a few hours, or her spilling whatever the hell she knows to the U.S. Government?"

The man with the ponytail stepped forward. "I'm sorry, boss, we did our best."

Petrovich mocked them. He cupped his hand around his ear and leaned in. "Apologies. I didn't hear that. You what? Are you saying you tried?"

Both men stood silent, bracing themselves for the looming storm of reprimand that was about to rain down upon them. Nikoli pointed to the man he didn't recognize. "You know—I don't even know who the fuck you are. Are you the one he recommended and was on the train? What's your name?"

"Yes, and it's Gregori, sir." He shifted from his left foot to his right.

Nikoli remained standing still. His blood reached its boiling point. He nodded several times and lowered his voice. Their eyes locked for several moments in a kind of silent struggle where each sized the other up. "You tried your best. Is that what you're telling me?"

The man dipped his chin and glanced toward the reflections on the parquet floor. Nikoli grabbed a book and threw it against the wall. "Fuck!" He opened a drawer and removed a pistol. Both men took a step back. Raw panic was in their eyes.

He stood for another few seconds, staring at the massive man, his face livid with rage. "Fuck you, Gregori!"

He pointed it at the man and squeezed the trigger. The expanding round punched a hole through his stomach. The splatter resembled a Rorschach inkblot, in the center of Gregori's belly. Dread was in his eyes. He grasped at the wound in desperation and fell back onto the cold, unforgiving floor, his eyes shut tight against the agony tearing through his body.

Petrovich strode around his desk and over to the dying man, who was lying on the ground grasping his gut. "It's a shame. Vasily spoke too highly of you, as well."

He fired two more rounds directly at his heart, killing him. Stepping over to Vasily, he pushed the muzzle under his chin while he pointed to Gregori with his other hand. A growl filtered through gritted teeth filled Vasily's ears. "Don't fucking think that can't be you."

Vasily fought the urge to wipe the spittle from his face. He swallowed hard. Petrovich pressed the barrel harder. "Give me just one solid reason you shouldn't join him, you dumb fuck. I relied on you, trusted you, and this is how you repay me."

Vasily gulped again. His sweat glistened in the light. "I—"

"Shut the fuck up."

Nikoli turned away and tossed his pistol onto his desk. It landed with a thump. "We're moving the timeline for the next test."

"To when?"

"Tomorrow."

"But I thought—"

Nikoli glared at his henchman. "You're thinking again."

"Sorry, sir."

Nikoli closed his eyes, took a deep breath, and exhaled slowly and deliberate. "At least tell me you got something off the laptop you took."

He sighed and swiveled his head, telegraphing his answer. "Sorry, but he wiped any trace of the email."

"Well, find her and uncover the location of the flash drive. We need to know what she knows."

"Yes, sir."

Nikoli stepped over to his bar and poured a shot of vodka into a glass.

"And Vasily?"

"Yes?"

He motioned toward the lifeless corpse on the floor. "Make a careful note of the body of your old friend. If you fuck things up this time, that'll be you." He slugged back the liquor and gestured at Gregori once more. "And clean this fucking mess!"

#

Pitor, one of the lead scientists for the High-Frequency Active Auroral array, entered Petrovich's office. He glanced down at the sizeable carpet rolled up on the parquet flooring. A blood stain seeped through the back. He stepped over the mess and approached the desk. "You wanted to see me about moving the test to tomorrow?"

Petrovich was attentive to Google Maps, zooming in and out of an undisclosed location. He turned to the scientist. "I did."

He watched as Pitor's eye's shifted to the pistol still lying on the top of his desk. He left it there. "We've had several discussions on where our following strike should be. We've had the most success targeting coastlines with nuclear power plants. Would you agree?"

"Yes, sir. That is correct."

"I have been looking at the Angra One plant in Brazil, and the Embalse one in Argentina, but I think after careful consideration, we will do Oslo. It will be much easier to stage for the Global Relief team since we've moved the timetable to tomorrow."

Pitor nodded and shifted his attention to the laptop monitor. "And the one after Oslo, sir? It appears you've already decided."

Petrovich turned and faced the laptop. "Yes, I have. It's time to make the West pay for what they did to my family. San Diego on Christmas will make an authoritative statement."

His lead scientist nodded his agreement. "Certainly, sir. It will."

Petrovich stared once more at the screen. Pitor cleared his throat. "So, sir. Same as last time? Closed for the day?" He formed air quotes with his fingers. "Company holiday? Essential personnel only?"

Petrovich nodded while he sat. "Yes. Send the memo immediately and start preparations."

"Yes, sir." Pitor pivoted and left the room. Petrovich swung the laptop back to face him and zoomed in over the San Diego area, studying it.

#

Stavenger Research Center

Stavenger, Norway
December 18th15:10 Local Time (14:10 GMT)
The computer's alarm went crazy. Erik Foss, one of the research analysts, rolled his chair from one monitor to the next. The phone rang. It was his boss. "What the hell is going on? I've got sensors going off everywhere around here?"

"I know. This is crazy! I'm registering a nine-point one quake."

"Nine-point-one? Where's the epicenter?"

"Uh, information is still coming in. Hold on." Erik slid his chair over to another monitor while he balanced the phone between his chin and shoulder. "Oh my God!"

"What? Where is it?"

There was a brief pause.

"Oslo."

13

CIA Headquarters
  Langley, VA
  December 18th
  09:30AM Local Time (14:30 GMT)

#

Blake MacKay parked his black Jeep Wrangler in his reserved spot in the underground parking garage at Central Intelligence Agency headquarters. It had been a week since he last visited to see his boss, Mike Brennan when he discussed what had happened to two little girls he'd rescued from a child sex trafficker.

The investigation led to a widespread underground empire in child sex exploitation. To date, over 300 people have been arrested, including several top Hollywood producers, actors, two senators and the heads keep rolling. Interpol has taken charge of the investigation and there is chatter some royals may face arrest. It amazed Blake how such evil can exist in the world.

He was pleased to find out that poor Roger didn't last long. Somebody shanked him while he was awaiting arraignment in the county lockup and died from his injuries. Of course, there were no cameras in the area it happened and no witnesses. Blake suspected it was a hit.

Blake strolled into the building and went to the top floor. His dark natural tan and chiseled features always garnered admiration from the women there; in particular, the younger ones who hadn't been there long and had never seen him before.

He heard them whisper *'who was that'* under their breath to their colleagues as he passed and would even catch an occasional silent *'wow'* on their lips. His ego loved the attention, but on the outside, he was portrayed as if he couldn't care less.

He entered the offices of Clandestine Affairs and approached the front desk.

He grinned at the young woman with the familiar face. "Hello, Jessica."

She glanced up and smiled as she flipped her long brown hair over her shoulder. "Good morning Mr. MacKay, it's been a while. How are you?"

"I am fine. You're looking lovely, as always." It warmed him to see her blush.

Blake pointed to his boss's office. "Are we in Mike's?"

"Uh, let me check." She turned to her monitor. "No. Conference room B today."

Blake strode along the hall and entered the cramped space. He frequently questioned why they would use a junior agent's office as a conference room.

Upon entering, he said his hellos to the usual players sitting at the round wood table. The Director of National Security, Veronica Slocum, a.k.a. "The Red Headed Bitch" as his handler, Mike Brennan, referred to her.

She and Mike butted heads constantly. Her belief in the power of diplomacy led her to hold liberal views, seeing violence as a last resort, only to be used when all other options had been exhausted.

Mike Brennan, Director of Clandestine Affairs, was Blake's boss. He reminded Blake of the character Cotton, the short, obstinate father of Hank Hill in the animated TV series "King of the Hill". Missing was Dr. Julian Thomas, the Director of the CIA. Mike had told Blake he was out of the country on *other business*, which was lingo for, *you don't need to know.*

On the wall was a flat panel monitor with someone Blake didn't recognize, connected via their secure video conferencing service.

Veronica stayed seated from across the table and nodded toward him. "Mr. MacKay. How are you?"

Blake turned to acknowledge her and smiled. "I'm fine Director. Thank you for asking."

After giving her a disapproving glance, Mike stood and extended his hand. "Blake. It's amazing you made it home safely. Outstanding job in Vienna, by the way. That Mossad operator really blew the shit out of that Zafar fellow." He followed with a wink.

Blake chuckled. "Thanks, Boss."

He understood what Mike was doing. The guy loved to be passive aggressive toward her, so this was his way of reminding Veronica of the victory of one of his more recent missions. He had to retrieve a high-ranking Iranian official before two other groups either kidnapped or killed his target. Using excessive force was necessary for achieving success.

The scowl Veronica returned to Mike was priceless, and there was no doubt he would receive a full ass-chewing for it later. Mike sat while Blake walked over and poured himself a glass of water.

Veronica started with introductions. "Blake, I'd like to introduce you to Marshal Reed. He is the sub-station chief in Moscow."

Blake laughed. "Oh, that's interesting. We have a sub-station in Moscow now?"

Veronica frowned. "Well—technically, no. It's a dry cleaner."

"Yeah, I figured as much." He sipped his drink.

Mike shook his head with a slight grin.

Blake focused his attention on the monitor and nodded. The station chief reciprocated.

"Mr. Marshal, why don't you bring Mr. MacKay up to date with what you know?"

"Thank you, Director."

He interjected. "Please, call me Blake." He pulled out a chair and sat next to Mike. "Hey, wait a minute." He turned to Mike. "Is this going to be about what we talked about in your office last week? Is this about the missing operative?"

Mike tapped his pencil on the table while he answered. "Yeah. I'll let Mr. Reed enlighten you and brief you. Mr. Reed, this is your show."

"All right. Well, two days ago we had an incident outside the embassy where a woman came running and asserted there were a couple of guys trying to kill her. Our security detail confirmed, in fact, there was gunfire a block away and two men sped off in a black

Mercedes after it collided with another car."

Blake raised his hand. "Sorry. I'm assuming there is something more to this. So far, this sounds like something for the locals."

"You're correct. The woman claimed to have some interesting information we would want to hear, and she didn't trust her government with the intel. So, we brought her in and listened to what she had to say."

Blake leaned back in his chair. "Okay. You have my attention. What did you find out?"

Mike grabbed a remote and switched on another monitor. The image of Nikoli Petrovich appeared on the screen and Veronica spoke.

"Blake, the gentleman you're looking at is Nikoli Petrovich. He is a Russian entrepreneur and philanthropist."

A picture of a man 6 feet tall, with dark hair and eyes. He was wearing a navy-blue V-neck sweater with gray slacks and was stepping into a black Bugatti Veyron.

Mike hit the table with both fists. "Bullshit. He's a goddamn psychopath!"

Veronica shifted her attention toward Mike. "It's possible, but unless we can prove otherwise, he's an entrepreneur and philanthropist. Now be silent until I'm finished."

Mike lifted a finger. "You left out, billionaire. He's also a billionaire."

As Mike and Veronica went back and forth, Blake could see the substation chief's face register confusion at the exchange.

"Don't worry, Mr. Reed; this is normal banter for them."

Veronica turned to Blake and raised her voice. "It is not, Mr. MacKay, and I'll ask you to do the same. Please be quiet so I can finish."

Blake glanced at Mike and opened his eyes wide while suppressing a smile. Mike did likewise as he tapped Blake's leg under the table with his foot.

"As I was saying—Mr. Petrovich is someone we've had our eyes on for some time. He has a massive research center in the middle of Siberia, and he has built a few things that have caught our attention."

Blake leaned forward. "Like what?"

Mike grabbed the remote again, clicked a button, and the image on the screen changed.

Veronica opened a folder and glanced down. "Are you familiar with

HAARP, Blake?"

"I am. It's something that can supposedly control the weather, right?"

"Not supposed, Blake. It can."

Blake's brow furrowed. "So, all those conspiracy whack-o's are correct?"

"In a manner of speaking. They're wrong about what our government wants to do with the technology. But with Mr. Petrovich—not so much."

"Okay, so what's this Petrovich guy doing with it?"

Mike pivoted to Blake. "That's something we're trying to figure out."

Blake turned his attention to Mike, who, in return, focused on the image in front of them. "Mr. Reed? This is your show."

"Thanks. Blake, the picture on the screen is the weather-controlling array Petrovich built. It's ten times larger than the one we have in Alaska. We sent an agent in to investigate, and he returned to us regular daily feedback with gaps of no more than thirty-six hours."

"And how long has it been since he last reported?"

"One week and counting."

Blake stood and paced around the table. "Okay, so we have a missing operative. What did you *think* this Petrovich guy was doing and what does this woman you talked about earlier have to do with this?"

Reed emphasized his concern. "We have suspected Petrovich was using it as a weapon. The woman here came in with some of the proof, and our absent spy has the rest. We think."

Blake tilted his head. "You think?"

Marshal sighed and closed his eyes. "Yeah. And this is partially my fault. We didn't send in an experienced field agent. Well, let me back up. He's trained but hasn't officially been given clearance for fieldwork. We got the impression from this woman that something significant was going to happen, and relatively soon."

He shifted his weight from one foot to the other. "We didn't have anyone available to go study the compound, so we sent him, Lance Tucker. I was reluctant, but didn't have any choice. It was supposed to be O F D only. Based on his other check-ins, he said he found some intriguing things and was piecing it together."

Blake's brow furrowed. "Hmmm, that is interesting. You said he was using it as a weapon? In what way?"

Veronica raised her hand. "I'm sorry. You said O F D? What's that?"

Mike smiled.

Marshal and Blake answered at the same time. "Observe from a distance."

Veronica nodded. "Thank you, Mr. Reed. Please continue."

"Right. We think he's causing natural disasters."

Blake scoffed. "Are you serious? How? And why would he do that?"

Veronica clicked her pen on the table. "It's three-fold. One. We have proof he held hundreds of millions of dollars in put options on the market. They were for various utility establishments and other high-tech companies whose headquarters were close to the shore. Remember the tsunami that leveled the Fukushima Power Plant and generated a massive disaster a couple of years ago?"

"Yes."

"We think he caused it to happen. When the near meltdown occurred, the company's stock dropped like a rock, as did many other high-tech outfits that were without electricity for days. Someone raked in over two-hundred and forty million dollars when they cashed in those puts."

Mike cocked his head and furrowed his brow. "Hold on a minute. I don't understand how that works. What in the hell is a put option?"

Veronica smirked. "Mike, it's a financial contract that gives the buyer the right to sell a particular asset at a predetermined amount of cash, called the strike price. But it has to be on or before a specified date. Put options are typically bought by traders who believe the share price of the company stock will decrease."

She brushed her palms together. "When it does, they offer it at the higher strike price and make a profit. The seller of the put option is contractually obligated to purchase the stock at the strike price if the buyer exercises the option. Petrovich is forcing the value to go down by causing these disasters."

Blake chuckled. "Didn't the bad guy in *Casino Royale* do the same thing? Except with an airline?"

Mike laughed. "Yeah, he did. I remember that now. That's probably where he got the idea."

Veronica's jaw tightened as she locked eyes on Mike's "It's not funny."

"Sorry."

"A similar event happened with the more recent earthquake and tsunami in Sri Lanka. Somebody made almost four hundred million."

"And you think it was Petrovich?" Blake opened his folder and jotted down some notes.

Veronica nodded. "Yes. We've now alerted all the world's markets, so if anyone tries this again, we can get a warning."

Blake turned back to Veronica. "You said three-fold."

"I'm getting to it." Veronica nodded to Mike, and he flipped to another image. This time it was of a massive Russian cargo plane with *Global Relief* painted on the side.

"Okay." She pointed at the plane. GR, as it's been called, is a disaster relief company also owned by Mr. Petrovich. He contracts with different governments to supply aid in the event of a natural catastrophe. He guarantees immediate help and is always the first to respond."

Blake rolled his eyes. "Gee, I wonder how he does that?"

"That's not all." Veronica jerked her thumb toward Mike. He switched to another picture. It was a split image of a huge solar collection array on the left and a massive ship on the right. The vessel had giant batteries on it and cables resembling tentacles coming out of the top and disappearing into the water.

"He has the largest solar collection array in the world. Next, he sells the power to the governments affected by the disaster. After it's all over, he makes an enormous profit from this operation. So, there's you're number three."

Blake shook his head. "Jesus Christ! This guy has the trifecta. He takes *find a need, fill a need* to a whole new level."

Mike nodded in agreement. "Except this guy is *the cause of the need, to fill the need*."

Blake agreed in return and shifted his focus back to the sub-station chief. "So, how does this woman fit into the picture?"

She's called Sofia Kuzma, and she worked for him for a few years, thinking he was developing a weather machine to produce rain in drought-hit parts of Africa.

Blake jotted down her name. "And what changed her mind?"

She said that she found evidence showing that the array was extremely active on days when it wasn't supposed to be used, as well as during natural disasters.

"Have they confirmed this?"

"That's the information she said she had, but hasn't produced yet. She also said some of Petrovich's thugs murdered a friend of hers and tried to kill her as well. All of this happened after she accessed some secure files on their network. He must have discovered the leak."

He adjusted the lapels of his jacket. "We verified the old college companion, the one she sent the data to, was killed and there were, in fact, two fellows chasing her when she ran to the embassy. They took off in a car, and after a brief investigation, we found it to be registered to a shell company owned by Petrovich."

"So, where is this woman now?"

"I'm getting there. She also claimed Petrovich shot our missing man."

Blake sat and put his hand on his forehead and rubbed it. He glanced back at Marshal Reed, Veronica, and then at Mike.

"So that's it? That's all we got? So, where is this woman?"

Marshal opened a file and perused it. "She's in a safe house here in Moscow."

Blake leaned in. "Why hasn't she given you the information?"

"She's been with us ever since she came to the embassy, and she won't tell us where it is. I think it's a matter of us gaining her trust. Which we don't have yet."

Blake turned to Mike. "I'll change her mind."

Mike nodded his agreement. "Mr. Reed, let us figure out the logistics on our end, and we'll contact you when Blake is on the way. You can expect him there sometime within the next twenty-four hours."

"Yes sir. I look forward to meeting you, Blake."

"Same here."

Mike disconnected the video call and reached for the receiver. He pressed a button and after a few seconds, someone answered. "Send in Alice."

Alice was a brilliant young inventor. He had been on loan to the CIA from DARPA, the Defense Advanced Research Agency, to field-test some of his technical inventions. However, the CIA found his innovative abilities too important to share.

What the CIA wants, the CIA gets, and they made Alice's tenure permanent with the promise they would transfer his achievements to

DARPA. Blake imagined there were some virtual fingers crossed behind the back of whoever from the CIA signed the paperwork.

Alice came into the room and sat next to Blake. Alice's, real name was Kyle Moran. He earned the nickname because of his strong affinity for his high school's basketball team, known as *The Alices*.

Alice topped the charts at six feet, eight inches and the chair appeared to be too small for him. He waved and gave an energetic, youthful smile. "Hi Blake."

"Hi Alice, whatcha got?"

Veronica cleared her throat. "Something to help you locate Agent Tucker."

Blake shifted his attention to Veronica.

She closed her folder. "That's the name of the operative who disappeared investigating Petrovich."

Alice smiled. "Sorry about the missing guy. Did you know him?"

Blake waved him off. "Don't worry about it, Alice. And no, I didn't know him."

Alice retrieved something from his pocket. "Anyway, we implanted a miniature capsule like this one under his skin." Alice handed Blake a tiny silver pellet.

"What's with all the James Bond references today? I'm assuming this is some kind of tracking contraption?"

Alice shook his head and smiled. "Oh no. This is much more. This is a data storage device and can store two terabytes. Whatever intelligence Agent Tucker gathered; he transferred it to a capsule similar to this one."

"And how is that done?"

"Via Bluetooth, with this." Alice handed Blake a phone. "There is a USB port where you transfer information, like video, images, etcetera, into the phone. Once you have the info uploaded, you can send it wirelessly to the device using an encrypted Bluetooth connection. It's limited in range to prevent any hacking, and the phone needs to be less than eight inches away to transfer the data."

Blake took the tiny object and examined it. "How does it get its power?"

"From the body's natural electric current."

"But what if he's—"

"Dead?" Alice nodded and cleared his throat. "Yes, you're correct,

Blake. If the carrier passes away, the only way to extract the data is to remove the object. Once we get power back to the item, we can extract it."

"I was going to say disappeared, but you know for a fact he's dead?"

Mike clasped his hands and rest them on the table. He sighed. "We do, Blake." Mike turned to Alice. "Sorry to interrupt. Go ahead."

"Right! Thanks Mike. The capsule turns into a beacon, but only if the agent activates it through a remote, or—if he's dead."

"There may be an obvious answer to this, and I think I know, but how does it know he's dead?"

"It loses its power source—a living body. It then triggers the beacon using a microscopic fuel cell."

"So why didn't the Moscow sub-station search for him as soon as the beacon went off?"

Alice's eyes shifted to Veronica. Blake followed suit. "Because they didn't know about it."

"And," Alice said, drawing out the word. "There's a bug."

"A bug?"

Alice sighed. "Yes. Agent Tucker was the first to receive the implant. Apparently, the transmitter isn't strong enough to burst through thick cloud cover. There have been heavy snow storms over the part of Siberia where he disappeared for the last week. The only way to find him is with an app I developed for your phone. It has a maximum range of five kilometers. Hand it to me now, and I'll install it for you."

Blake handed it to him. "Ok, anything else I need to know?"

Alice fiddled with Blake's phone while he spoke. "Yes. The battery has a life of nine—perhaps ten days from the time it's activated. I'm hoping the cold climate will extend the battery life to give you more time."

Mike opened a bottle of water. "Based on when we know Agent Tucker disappeared, you have a window of forty-eight to sixty hours to find him. Assume fifty."

"Got it." Blake wrote in his notes.

Veronica's mobile rang. She answered and listened to the caller. Her eyes widened. "What? When? Ok, thank you."

Mike swallowed his drink. "What is it?"

"There's been an earthquake off the coast of Norway. A tsunami wiped out their nuclear power plant in Oslo. No word on the number of fatalities yet, but they expect it to be high."

Mike's forehead creased. "Any observations on the state of the reactor?"

She shook her head. "No. Not at the moment."

Mike stood and pushed in his chair. "With this fresh development, we've gotta move now." He turned to his number one agent. "Blake—helo is waiting to take you to the airport."

Veronica closed her folder and also got to her feet. "We're not sure this is the work of Petrovich."

Mike scoffed. "My ass it isn't. You need to stop being so naïve."

Anticipating a sharp retort from Veronica, Blake quickly interjected, trying to defuse the situation. "I've got my go-bag in the back of my Jeep."

Blake rose and Mike held out his hand. "Best of luck, Blake. We'll talk while you're in the air."

Veronica and Alice extended the same well wishes. Blake hustled to the garage and got his pack out of his Jeep and ran out to the helipad.

14

CIA Safe-House
    Moscow, Russia
    10:00AM (06:00 GMT)
    December 19th

#

Arriving in Moscow on a commercial flight from Poland, the CIA's top clandestine agent made his way through customs using fake credentials. The station chief left a car for him at the airport. As usual, they packed the trunk with goodies, including a 9mm Glock with amble ammunition.

Blake drove the nondescript sedan to the safe house on Moscow's Northeast side. The landscape was gray, and the temperature was cold. Dirty snowbanks lined the streets with a cap of fresh powder from early morning snow. The wiper blades left streaks on the cracked windshield and hindered his view. Blake's breath created wispy patterns inside, adding to the fog on the windscreen. He dialed the thermostat to high and hit the dash a fourth time, trying to get the heater working.

"Piece of shit."

He glanced at his GPS. Being less than a kilometer away, he abandoned his effort at warming the interior. A quick drive-by revealed nothing out of the ordinary, so he continued two more blocks, traveled west, drove to the next street, and went north. After a couple more turns, Blake veered off to the side of the road and waited for three minutes.

He peeked at his mirrors for any kind of tail, then headed back in the direction he came. One hundred meters past the rear of the home, he stopped and paused again. Confident nobody had tailed him, he shifted to park, checked his weapon to make sure a round was chambered, got out of the vehicle and walked toward the safe-house.

The previous evening, two men drove Sofia to the location. Oscar and Sam were assigned to the Moscow office eighteen months ago. Their personalities were polar opposites. Oscar, a former offensive lineman for the University of Michigan, was from the inner city of Detroit, while Sam, a collegiate lacrosse player, studied computer science at Duke. The duo possessed a unique set of skills and together they were a formidable team.

They made the introductions to the group of agents on the detail to protect her until Blake arrived.

"Ma'am. We're going to leave you now. You're in expert care with these gentlemen. You have our number; in case you need anything."

"Thank you." Sofia shook their hands. The two men smiled. Oscar gave her a reassuring pat on the shoulder while he presented her with a card.

"This has all of our contact information. I know you wrote it down, but keep this in your purse as a backup."

Grasping the card, she nodded. A tall agent in his mid-thirties approached her.

"Hi Sofia, I'm Roger." He motioned for her. "Come on, I'll give you a quick tour of the place so you can get your bearings."

Located in the heart of the block, the quaint home exuded a cozy ambience with its humble proportions. Built after World War II as part of a rebuilding project, it sat among other homes of a similar style and size. The interior layout followed a conventional design: a modest living and dining room in front with a kitchen and bathroom in the rear. It had two staircases to the second floor: one from the foyer and the other from the kitchen at the back of the house.

After the tour, Roger introduced Derek and Trent, the cook of the group. Finishing her dinner, she helped with the dishes to keep her mind off of the events of the previous days. She spent the rest of the evening reading in her room and went to bed.

#

The next morning, Sofia was seated at the farmhouse-style table with a cup of hot tea. She gazed out the window, contemplating all she'd been through the past few days. One of the field operatives, noticing her demeanor, pulled back a chair and attempted to make her feel more comfortable.

"Miss Kuzma?"

Sofia grasped the cup with both hands, more out of comfort than to keep them warm. She glanced at the agent.

"Ma'am, we have one of our best agents coming here to take care of you." He placed his hand on her wrist as he spoke. "His name is Blake MacKay."

Sofia's eyes met his, and she smiled.

"By the way, in case you've forgotten, I'm called Roger. Derek, Trent and I are here for your protection. We won't let anything happen to you."

Trent stood at the stove and prepared breakfast while Derek poured himself a glass of orange juice.

"Bacon. There's plenty if anyone wants some." The master cook held a piece between his fingers and shoved it into his mouth. He wiped the grease across the floral-patterned apron he chose to wear.

A knock on the front door startled everyone.

"What the hell?" Roger rose and drew his pistol, motioning for Trent to take their asset upstairs.

He snapped his fingers and whispered, "Derek!" then motioned him toward the living room window. "Check it out."

Her voice rose and became shrill. Her body tensed and she hunched her shoulders. "What is it? What's going on?"

Trent nudged her toward the back staircase. "Just precautions, ma'am. It may be Agent MacKay, but I need you to move faster."

Derek peered through the curtains and glanced out onto the wooden porch. He made a mental note of the one woman but continued to scan the yard and street.

"It's some woman. Just herself from what I can see. She's wearing a coat with the logo of that real estate company we see all over town."

Roger checked his weapon. "Well, get rid of her."

"Yep."

He opened the door and said hello in his finest Russian.

Her eyes widened, and her lips curled up. "Oh, an American."

He lied. "Canadian actually. Was my Russian accent that bad?"

She smiled once more. "No, it's fine. My name is Freda Romanoff. Do you own—"

Raising his hands, he did his best to ward off the sales pitch. "Let me stop you right there. This isn't my home. I'm watching the house for a friend while he is away on holiday. I don't think—"

She nodded and continued to show her friendly face. "I understand. You don't have to say another word. However, would you mind if I left a brochure for the homeowner? These properties are extremely popular, and we could get him prime money."

Anything to make you go away.

He held out his hand. "I suppose."

She reached into her coat, drew a silenced pistol, and shot Derek through the heart.

His eyes went wide as he grasped his chest. As he leaned over, she pushed the tip of the barrel against the top of his head and squeezed two more rounds.

Roger felt the thump of Derek's body hitting the floor and the familiar noise of the spent casings as they bounced on the porch.

A burly man appeared behind her. She turned to him and pressed her finger to her lips, then whispered into his ear. "Alexei, take the back door. I'll enter from here."

In the kitchen, Roger stood and squeezed his back against the wall. His heart raced. He slid down to a crouch to make himself a smaller target. A quick peek toward the foyer revealed nothing.

An enormous figure, dressed in black, barged through the back door.

He spun and raised his weapon, but Alexei was too fast.

He grabbed Roger's arm and pointed the pistol skyward. A round went into the ceiling and an elbow smashed into his nose, breaking it.

Alexei smacked Roger's arm into the wall three times and forced him to drop his gun.

Training took over, and the agent retaliated. His adrenaline gave him a burst of strength. He front-kicked his assailant onto the table. Roger lunged forward and rammed both fists into the huge man's chest. Alexei kneed Roger in the belly, stood and connected to his jaw with a swift right cross. The impact hurled him into the kitchen wall. Pans rattled and fell from where they hung. Alexei rammed his fist into Roger's midsection.

Gasping for breath, he fought back. He cupped his palms and slapped them over Alexi's ears, rupturing his eardrums. As Alexei screamed out in pain, he put his hands to his ears. Roger returned the favor with three rapid punches to the stomach and a right elbow to the jaw.

The impact slammed the intruder back against the stove. Alexi grabbed the skillet and threw scalding bacon grease at Roger, who screamed as it burned his face and eyes.

With both hands on the pan, Alexei swung at Roger. It bashed him on the side of the skull and knocked him out cold. Gasping for breath, Alexei tossed the makeshift weapon to the ground and recovered Roger's pistol. Without hesitation, he shot him in the head.

#

Sofia's eyes were wide. She trembled as Trent spoke to her.

"Calm down. You'll give away our position." He reached to his ankle and yanked out his AMT backup, a.380 caliber automatic with eight rounds. He handed it to Sofia, backed her into an upstairs bedroom, and pushed her toward the closet.

"It's loaded." He showed her the safety lever. "See this? Flip it down, then point and squeeze the trigger." After he shut the door, he crept toward the door and listened out into the hallway.

Alexei had blood on his face. His coat was torn, and he fought to catch his breath. He locked eyes with Freda. the onetime female KGB agent, through the kitchen doorway. She stood near the other steps and signaled for him to ascend the back stairs midway and wait for her signal.

Keeping his back to the wall as he went, he stopped when he caught sight of her across the hall, on the front staircase. She hand-signaled him the American's location. An ex-Spetsnaz himself, he understood the technique for situations like this. When he got the sign, he shuffled his feet on the stairway.

Trent darted out of the bedroom and aimed his pistol over the rail toward Alexei. He didn't notice Freda on the front staircase, and two silent rounds blew out the side of his skull.

The two met at the top, in the hallway. "Excellent shot."

She nodded. "Where is she?"

"I don't know. Start looking."

They searched the nearest bedroom. First, under the bed, then the wardrobe and for hidden rooms in the walls.

Sofia stayed crouched behind the safety of the closed closet door of the farthest room. The sound of each step they took echoed like a pounding heartbeat, a haunting reminder of impending doom approaching her.

It was dark, and she was sweating. She heard the shaking in her voice as she exhaled. Grasping the pistol with both hands, she shut her eyes and took slow, deep breaths.

#

Blake was a block away. Walking along the alley behind the line of homes, he checked his watch, continually scanning the space for signs of anything unusual.

As he got closer to the house, the backdoor stood open. Pulling his Glock from his waistband, he ran to the doorway. He ducked his head in and out of the kitchen for a quick peek. A body lay sprawled on the floor. He dashed into the house, weapon up, and scanned the room.

Keeping his pistol at the ready, he went to the corpse lying on the ground. Not knowing who he was, he identified him as American from his features and clothing. Blake felt for a pulse but abandoned the effort when he noticed the placement of the bullet hole. The sound of footsteps and voices echoed from the rear stairwell.

He stood and crept to the back stairs. Not seeing the bacon grease, his foot slid and hit the table leg, causing it to scoot across the tiles.

Shit!

Freda stopped and raised her hand. She snapped her fingers twice. Alexei froze and waited for her orders. She pointed her index finger in the direction of the floor and wiggled three times, then a quick nod of her head. His partner motioned his understanding.

Blake tip-toed out of the kitchen and into the hallway at the front of the house. He checked the two rooms and aimed his weapon toward the staircase as he scanned the dining room. Satisfied the bottom level was clear, he started back to the kitchen to take the other staircase.

With his shoulders pressed to the wall, he stepped back into the kitchen. The opening to the stairs was a few feet away. He took a deep breath and in one quick movement; he positioned himself in the stairwell. It wasn't what he expected. A foot slammed into his chest and propelled him into the frame of the back door.

Alexei attacked. The force of the kick knocked Blake's gun out of his hand. He raised his arms in a defensive move and thwarted the attack. He pushed his assailant off and pushed him into the wall next to the stairs.

Blake rammed his head into Alexei's midsection and then drove upward, mashing the top of his skull with the bottom of the man's jaw. His attacker grabbed his lapels and threw him into the wall on his left. The massive man latched onto a chair. Recognizing what was about to happen and not having enough time to get out of the way, Blake took a defensive posture and waited. Alexi broke it over his back. Shards of wood cracked and splintered in all directions.

He spun Blake around, catching him with a hard right cross on his cheek.

Blake drove his heel into Alexei's foot and pushed him back. With his attacker away from him, he ripped the drawer from the cabinet and flung its contents in the huge man's direction. Silverware crashed to the floor.

#

Freda entered the third bedroom and eyed the closet. She moved toward the door with muted steps. With her weapon drawn, she yanked the door open. Sofia pointed the AMT and tried to squeeze the trigger. Nothing happened.

Freda smirked, glancing at the safety latch. "*Dura, ti s predohranitelya ne snyala!*" She grabbed the pistol from Sofia's hands and put it in her pocket. She snatched a handful of hair and jerked her out of the closet.

Sofia protested. "No!"

"Shut up." She backhanded Sofia. "Stay there or I kill you."

The commotion coming from downstairs was relentless. She held the gun on Sofia as she leaned toward the door and shouted, "Hurry and kill him! I found her."

Sofia spotted a tall leaded glass vase on the desktop next to her. Without hesitating, she grabbed it, swung hard, and broke her assailant's arm. The weapon hit the floor, and the assassin screamed in pain. Sofia tried to run past her, but Freda stretched out her other arm and latched on to her clothing. The woman was strong and swung her back into the room.

"You bitch! You broke my arm."

Freda side kicked her in the gut. It threw her back against the bed. The former Spetsnaz grabbed the vase and came at her. Sofia rolled out of the way, but not far enough. The well-trained FSB agent was too quick, even with a broken arm. She swept Sofia's feet out from under her and made her fall to the floor.

She yelled in pain as her attacker kicked her in the ribs four times. She turned around and went for her pistol. Sofia struggled to her feet and grabbed an empty, hard-sided suitcase. She raised it above her head and slammed it over the back of her assailant's head. The woman hit the floor. The gun she took slid out of her pocket and onto the rug.

Sofia dove for the weapon. Freda latched on to her ankle with her uninjured hand and pulled to hold her back. Sofia smashed her foot into Freda's side and grabbed the gun.

"The safety's off now. *Sdohni, suchka!*"

She squeezed the trigger.

#

Blake grasped the drawer with both hands and demolished it across Alexei's face with a strong backhand. The impact threw him back. Blood flowed from a deep gash next to his left eye. As he went, he tripped backward over Roger's corpse. He attempted to stand. Blake leaped over and drove his knee into the bleeding man's forehead.

They were beside the refrigerator. Blake opened the door and positioned his foe's head inside the frame and slammed the door on it four times. Blood trickled from his ears.

He stopped when multiple shots came from the top floor. Scurrying over to the door, he grabbed his Glock, turned, and delivered two rounds into the assassin. Once in the chest, the other through the face. Blood splattered and trickled down the refrigerator.

He dashed upstairs with his weapon drawn. The distant sound of a woman's sorrowful weeping echoed from the farthest bedroom. When he entered, Sofia pointed the pistol at her rescuer and pulled the trigger.

He ducked back out of the room. The next shot hit the wall opposite the room, followed by the familiar click of an empty pistol locking its slide open.

Sofia was crying. "Don't come in here. I'll shoot you."

He shouted from the hallway, "Sofia! It's Blake MacKay. I'm here to take you somewhere safe. I'm stepping into the room. My hands are empty."

He edged around the corner with his hands raised. Sofia stood over Freda's lifeless body. When he entered the room, she ran to him, embraced him, and sobs racked her body. Surprised and not expecting this. All he could do was comfort her.

"It's okay. You're safe now." He patted her on the back, but she continued to cry. With compassion, he softly grasped her shoulders and pushed her away. Their eyes met, and he wiped away her tears.

"Sofia. It's okay."

With complete submission, she fell into his arms and wept.

Blake stroked her back again. "Come on. Let's get you outta here."

15

Moscow, Russia
10:45 AM (6:45 GMT)
December 19th

#

Holding her arm to help keep her steady, Blake guided Sofia down the stairs. She had a slight limp after her fight with the assassin, and the walk to the central floor proved difficult. "Okay, one last step. I'll get you over to a chair where you can sit down."

When they reached the bottom of the back staircase, He released her. "Hold the rail."

She gasped as she saw the destruction in the kitchen and Roger's body. "Oh, my God!" Sorrow filled her eyes. She started to cry and mumbled while she covered her mouth with her hand. Tears ran down her face as she pointed to Roger. "He's, he's dead."

Blake thought for a proper response, but the only thing coming out was, "Yeah."

"But I, I was just talking to him a few minutes ago." With her head swiveling back and forth, she searched the area for any signs of the others. "Where are Trent and Derek?"

He sighed and placed his hand on her shoulder. "I'm afraid they're dead, too."

Both hands went to her face. Her breath caught in her throat. "Who killed Roger?"

"Roger Rabbit?" He chuckled and smiled, hoping to lighten the mood.

Her eyes met his and her brow furrowed. "What? No, asshole."

Well, humor didn't work.

Blake motioned with his chin. "I'm sorry. It was in poor taste. Probably the guy there."

She turned toward the refrigerator and gasped again. "Oh, holy shit! Who killed him?"

"I did."

Sofia's gaze swept up and down his body, uncertainty etched on her face. She couldn't quite decipher the enigmatic aura he exuded, leaving her on edge.

"Stay there a second." Stepping over to the table, he pulled out a chair and went back to get her, kicking clutter to make a path along the way. Blake helped her navigate around all the things scattered about the kitchen floor from his fight with Alexei. She placed her arm on the tabletop to shift the weight from her foot and sat in the seat.

"Are you going to be all right? I need to make sure there aren't any other people here."

She nodded and forced a smile. "Yeah. I'll be fine."

"Okay. Wait here." He left the kitchen, heading for the front of the house. Pulling back the curtains, he scanned out of the window for signs of anyone waiting outside. He walked back to talk to Sofia. "Do you have a phone?"

"Uh…"

She searched the room through the clutter on the floor when she spotted her purse.

"Yes." She rose to a stand, taking care to navigate the scattered debris lying around as she picked her way through the mess to reach it. Wincing at the sharp twinge in her side, she lifted it from its resting place. Blake snatched it from her and rummaged through it until he found what he was looking for.

She scrunched her nose and wrinkled her brow. "Hey! You could ask for it. I would have given it to you."

Rummaging in her bag, he ignored her. "It's amazing how you women can ever answer a call with all the shit you carry around."

After removing her phone, he dropped it on the floor and handed her the purse. He stomped on the device until he spotted what he wanted.

She sucked in several deep breaths to calm herself and then burst out. "Hey! What the hell did you smash my phone for?"

Blake sifted through the pieces until he located the SIM card. He grabbed it and snapped it in half, holding the broken fragments inches from her face. He shook it in front of her nose. "This is how they discovered you. I'm making sure they don't get hold of you again."

"Couldn't you have just taken the card out and let me keep the telephone?"

"No! They could still track you. Even if it's off. Trust me. This is what I do. But, as I said, they're not going to grab you on my watch. Come on."

He latched onto her arm and helped her through the door and out into the back alley. "I've got a car a couple of blocks away. Is your leg ok or do I need to carry you?"

Sofia stopped walking. "I can damn well walk, thank you. And I can do it without your help."

Blake liked her tenacity but didn't want to give anything away. "Suit yourself." He continued to stride in front of her, increasing the distance between them at his pace.

She called out. "Hey! I said I could walk. I didn't say I could run a marathon. Slow down."

With a smile on his face, he reached the automobile and opened the door for her. She shot him another disapproving glare.

Blake grinned. "Just behaving like a gentleman. Don't read too much into it."

Circling around to the driver's side, he scanned his surroundings one more time. Satisfied they weren't being watched, he stepped into the car and sped off with Sofia. One block down, on the opposite side of the street, Vasily sat waiting.

#

"Okay, got it." Blake ended his call.

He turned to Sofia. "It was Marshal Reed, the man you met at the embassy. He has someplace else for us to go."

"Will it be safe?"

Blake smirked. "Yes, because now they can't track you."

It amazed him. The incompetence of those idiots for not checking if she had her phone. One stupid mistake cost them their lives, but he wouldn't let Sofia know. With all she'd been through, he didn't want her to feel responsible for the deaths of three more individuals.

He grinned and laughed out loud. "Die you bitch."

She whirled to face him, her tone seething with anger. "Excuse me?"

Blake chuckled again at her expression. "It's what you yelled before you shot holes in the woman back there."

As she beamed, she radiated her beauty, and it impressed him. It was the first time he'd paid any proper attention to her. Her smile drew him in as her charcoal lashes fluttered to her cheeks, his gaze finally resting on her full lips.

Appearing to be less tense, she turned to face the front. "So, you speak Russian?"

He wiped the inside of the windshield with his arm. "Enough to know you were angry as hell."

They both giggled, and it helped relieve the tension.

Blake hit the dash again. He glanced over at Sofia and pointed to it. "The damn heater."

"It might be it's your fuse?"

Blake studied his rearview mirror. "Yeah, perhaps. I'll have to check."

The black Mercedes several cars back caught his eye, and he put it in the back of his mind. He made a left turn onto the next major street and checked the mirror again. "So, tell me how this array thing works. I've seen pictures of it and read a brief description, but I'm not a hundred percent sure what it does."

Sofia bit her lip and hesitated. "Um."

"Come on, I need to know. If I have to, all I've gotta do is call our HAARP program in Alaska and get detailed files. You're not telling me anything I don't already have access to. But you'd be speeding up the process. So, let's go. Spill it out."

"So, you say you have seen photos?"

Blake nodded and checked the mirror again. "Yes."

"Assuming you viewed pictures, did you notice the many antennae present?"

"Of course." His eyes danced back and forth between the mirror and out the windshield.

"Those individual antennae are IRI's, or ionospheric research instruments. They're radio frequency transmitters. Combined, we can put a tremendous amount of energy through them, and we can disturb an area of the ionosphere."

A broad smile crossed her face. "We can change the weather and make it rain in certain areas. I worked on making it focus a more intense beam so the precipitation chances would increase and the accuracy of where we wanted the rain to fall would also improve."

"I feel a 'but' coming on," smiled Blake. He glanced again into the rearview. The Mercedes was still pursuing them. Not wanting to alarm Sofia, he kept her talking. "Keep going. Fascinating stuff." He turned right at the upcoming corner and went straight.

"Yes. A massive but. All of it was a ruse. The array was never able to make it rain anywhere."

He scratched his nose while searching in the mirror for the tail. "So, why did you think he was making it rain?"

"He simulated a Doppler radar screen, making us believe it was real. Also, the video he showed us was all fake too. The video was of some village in Africa. It showed all these lovely plants growing and families eating the fresh vegetables they grew."

She adjusted in her seat.

"I found out they used massive tanker trucks with hoses on extended booms to spray non-potable water in the air to simulate rain. Enormous screens blocked out the sun. It resembled a movie set for a major motion picture. They trucked in and planted living plants to show how Petrovich's 'weather machine' performed the miracle of life-giving rain."

Blake made another turn and immediately checked his mirror. "Wow. That's pretty amazing. I bet he spent a pretty penny on all of that."

"Hell no. The cheap bastard. He was able to do it for the cost of a couple of truckloads of rice and a thousand cases of bottled water. If I had to guess, if you went back there now, all you'd see is dead plants and plastic bottles scattered about."

"So, is that some of the information that you found? What else do you have?"

"Yes, I have that proof and there's more."

The Mercedes turned with them, three cars back.

"Okay, I'm following you. What then?"

"Well, apparently, Mr. Petrovich put vastly more energy through it than I knew about. Disrupting the ionosphere with so much power causes a significant shift in the pressure streams."

"I understand. What's that do?"

"Well, when you make such a dramatic difference in the pressure streams, the jet streams alter and create a huge downstream. When the downstream occurs, and if it's oversized, it can cause an earthquake."

Blake made another right turn at the oncoming corner. "It just doesn't seem possible to me. Are you certain Petrovich is responsible for this?"

She stiffened in her seat and turned to gaze forward. "I know he's doing it. I have proof."

Blake peeked over at Sofia. "And you have this evidence hidden somewhere?"

She twisted and peered out the side window. "Yes."

He glanced in his mirror and spotted the black Mercedes. The light in front of them went red. Too many cars had driven into the intersection from the opposite direction. Blake braked to a stop, first in line. His eyes flashed to the mirror and his fingers curled tight, holding onto the steering wheel. "I don't want you to panic, but we've got a tail."

She moved her head. "Don't move. Use your side mirror. Black Mercedes, second car back."

Sofia gasped. "I think it's Vasily. He works for Petrovich. He's the leader of the rest of them, and he's the man who tried to kill me."

She fidgeted in her seat. "What are you going to do?"

Blake smiled and twisted around to her. "Calm down. Trust me." The light went to green, and Blake kept his foot on the brake. The two lanes of traffic on either side of them moved. After a few seconds, horns blared.

Blake put his hands in the air to signal to the people behind him he had a problem. Horns blared again. He raised his index finger, hoping they would understand and wait a moment longer. Blake focused on the light.

"Come on."

Sofia's brow furrowed. "What are you doing? You're angering people."

Blake smiled and fidgeted with the dial on the radio and the gearshift. More horns blared. People yelled at him in Russian. Blake glanced back at the light. "Come on, you fucking light."

Blake used the side mirror to keep an eye on the driver in the vehicle behind him. The door opened, and the man stepped to the pavement, cursing in Russian. He marched forward, fists clenched. Blake's foot hovered over the gas pedal. As the motorist reached his rear fender, Blake revved the engine as his eyes concentrated on the light. The man strode back and got into his auto.

Focused back on the light, it turned yellow. He tried to reassure her. "Hold on tight and don't panic."

With eyes wide, Sofia turned her head to the rear. "What? What are you doing?"

"Turn back around. You have to stay calm. I'm going to lose this tail."

He shifted to reverse and floored it. With his foot on the gas, he rammed into the automobile behind him. The force of the collision slammed the car behind into the front of the black Mercedes.

The light turned red. Blake changed into first gear and tore off through the intersection.

The impact pinned Vasily's Mercedes between two cars. He thrust his foot to the floor. The Mercedes forced the smaller car out of the way, but the traffic was heavy. Cars filled both lanes on either side of him and traffic at the crossing intersection was six lanes across and busy with vehicles. Vasily slammed his fist down on the wheel as Sofia and the unknown man drove away.

16

Langley, VA
    December 19th
    02:10 AM (07:10 GMT) 12:10 PM Moscow

#

Mike Brennan mashed the end button on his mobile phone. "God Dammit!" Another call in the middle of the night and another emergency that couldn't wait. It was par for the course and part of the job, and he accepted it.

He stepped out of bed, got dressed and fixed himself a coffee before heading to CIA Headquarters. On the way, he dialed his office from the car. They had explicit instructions on what he wanted, and he demanded the information be on his desk when he arrived. If they failed, there would be hell to pay. Then he called the National Security Director, Veronica Slocum. He was all too pleased to awaken her in the middle of the night.

A sleepy voice answered. "Hello."

"I got a call from Marshal Reed a few minutes ago. Do you know what your fucking *entrepreneur* and *philanthropist,* Petrovich, did?"

"What? Is this Mike? Of course not. I was sound asleep. What are you rambling on about?"

"I'll tell you what I'm talking about. The asshole sent armed assassins to the safe house in Moscow. They killed a trio of our finest agents."

"What about Miss Kuzma? Is Blake okay?"

He pounded the top of the steering wheel with his palm. "Are you shittin' me? Veronica! Did you listen to what I said? Three of our men! They're all gone, and your first reaction is to ask me about this woman?"

"Yes, I heard you. I'm sorry to hear about losing those operatives. There's nothing we can do about it now, so we need to focus on the task at hand. What happened to—Sofia?"

Mike turned onto the next street. "She's fine. Our asset walked in on the attack and killed the fuckers. He has the woman now and they are en route to another location."

"By *our asset*, I assume you mean Blake. So, what are you doing now?"

He took a swig of his coffee. "I'm on my way to the office. And yes, I was talking about Blake. I've asked them to get me everything they know about Petrovich. We need to know where he lives, where he drinks when he takes a shit and anything he has scheduled on his calendar for the next three months. They're supposed to have it when I get there."

"And what do you plan to do with the information?"

"Seriously? What the fuck do you think I'll do with it? Get our asset in and take his ass out."

"No. do nothing until I can examine all the intel and make a rational decision. I'll be there as soon as I can."

Mike drew in a deep breath and released it. "No. You can go back to sleep. I'll fill you in later this morning. There's nothing more that can be done with both of us there. You should at least get some shuteye."

There was a brief pause before she responded. Her voice was warmer and almost friendly in its tone. "Ok. Thank you. But I need you to let me know what you find out ahead of any proceedings. Do nothing until it's been authorized. This Petrovich character might be more politically connected than we thought. Taking him out could have some grave consequences regarding national security and diplomatic relations with the Kremlin."

He took another slow sip of coffee, hoping the silence would make her uneasy. "Do you understand?"

He smiled. "Yeah, fine. You'll get a full report in the morning. Don't worry."

"Thank you." She disconnected.

Mike's intentions were different. He hoped she appreciated his 'simple act of kindness' but in reality, he hated her and didn't want her getting in his way. By the time he finished his call with Veronica, he'd arrived at CIA headquarters. He took the elevator to the control center and made his presence known. He pushed the door open with extreme prejudice. "Okay folks, what have you got for me?"

#

Blake sped along the busy street, away from the accident he caused. He took his first right, followed by the second left. The engine of the tiny auto wailed as he red-lined it before shifting gears.

Sofia turned to him. "I can't believe what you just did. Why would you hit the man's motorcar?"

Blake's brow furrowed as he shifted his gaze from Sofia to the road ahead. "What? Are you serious? I pinned your buddy Vasily between those two cars. He was following you and I had to lose the tail, and it's what I did."

"But the other man. What about him?"

Rolling his eyes, he shook his head in disbelief. "I don't get you. You have assassins after you. They already killed a friend of yours and three of my colleagues and you're worried about some other guy's car?"

Downshifting, he slowed to make another turn and accelerated again. "Listen up, gal, in this business, you know what they call it?"

She didn't answer. "Hmm? It's called collateral damage. I did what I had to do to get the job done, and my task is to keep you safe. I don't apologize for it. Got it?"

She remained focused on the windscreen.

"Got it?"

"Sofia?"

She waved her arm dismissively. "Okay. I get it. Sorry, I brought it up. Where are we going?"

Blake had another peek in his rearview mirror as he responded. "Change of plans. We're ditching this wagon."

He made five more turns before he found a sufficient place to leave the auto. Heading into an extensive gravel-packed lot, He parked behind a trash dumpster, making the car hidden from view. Retrieving a rag out of the back seat, he began wiping off everything inside the vehicle, then handed the towel to Sofia.

"Wipe anything you've touched. Open the door with the cloth and get out."

"Why? There are cameras at each intersection and—"

"Because I said so! Do it!"

When they were out of the car, Blake grabbed the towel from her and wiped the outside door handles and trunk. As he was cleaning the trunk, he turned to Sofia. She was standing still, with a blank stare on her face.

"Listen up. I do stuff and ask you to do things for a reason. If you want to stay alive, don't question me. And so you know, cameras don't help them with this old scrap heap. It appears to be a piece of shit, and from all outward appearances, it is. However, there's been some money put into it." A smile tugged at the corners of his mouth. "The tag and registration are fake, and let's say there have been modifications to the glass, making the cameras worthless. They would only know who was in this car if they found fingerprints and they were in the database."

He finished wiping the trunk. "Okay? Make sense now?"

Sofia was quiet. "Hey! Miss Kuzma. Got it?"

"Yes! Sure, I've got it! Now can we go?"

He kept the towel and stepped toward her. He took Sofia's hand and walked her at a hurried pace to the nearest busy intersection. Blake hailed a taxi. When they got in, he instructed their cabbie. After about thirty minutes, he told the driver to pull over. He paid the fare, plus a generous tip, and he and Sofia exited the car. They were in the middle of a block, less than one kilometer from Red Square.

Surveying her surroundings, her brow furrowed. "What are we doing here?"

Blake grabbed her hand. "Come on."

They strolled for several blocks and then diverted onto Neglinnaya Street. The Ararat Park Hyatt Hotel was in view. They ambled into the underground garage, and Sofia stopped cold. He pivoted to face her. He shrugged, opened his eyes wide, and held out his palms. "What are you waiting for? Come on!"

"Where are we going? What are we doing here?"

Blake rolled his eyes and sighed. He took a step toward her, put his right hand on her shoulder, and took a deep breath. "Listen—we've got a trust issue going on here." He waved his other index finger back and forth between himself and her. "You've got important information we need—which you haven't given us yet. We've also let you in on a few details you're not supposed to know."

Sofia scoffed and brushed Blake's hand off her shoulder, folding her arms in front of her. "Like what?"

"The fact the CIA operates here, and we have safe houses, among other matters. How do we know you won't go to your government and reveal all this to them?"

"Because I don't trust them! I have people trying to kill me."

"Bingo! Remember—you came to us, honey, and at this moment, I'm the only person you've got. This is a two-way street and right now, we're not feeling it."

Blake turned to walk away when Sofia blurted out from behind him. "But you've already lied to me once."

He stopped and swung back to face her. "Huh? When?"

"You said you spoke a little Russian, but you expressed yourself to the cab driver in near perfect Russian."

"Listen, I've been speaking—wait, *near* perfect? Please." Blake drew out the word with a tone of playful arrogance.

She giggled.

He backed off the diatribe he was about to deliver and smiled back. He put his hand back on her shoulder. "You have got to have some faith in me. You're living in my world now where things are not what they appear, and you're limited to who you can trust. And, right now, I'm the only one you've got, ok?"

She gave a mock salute and nodded.

"Fine. Stay here for a moment."

Blake went to the attendant's office, showed the attendant a fake ID, and got the keys to a vehicle. He waved Sofia over and they walked deeper into the garage. They went to a level full of luxury automobiles, Lamborghinis, Ferraris, Bugattis, Bentleys and much more.

He hit the button on the key fob and listened for the chirp of the car unlocking. Parked three stalls away was a black Mercedes Benz Brabus 850 6.0 iBusiness.

With wide eyes and a smile, Sofia nodded. "Wow! What is this?"

He grinned from ear to ear. "This—is motoring perfection. Beneath the hood is an SV12 Biturbo, delivering eight-hundred and fifty horsepower and can go from zero to sixty in under four seconds. The top speed is two-hundred and seventeen miles per hour. It's packed with multiple computers, five monitors, two printers—and its own Wi-

Fi spot. This bad puppy has everything we need to get you out of the country in one piece. Plus, it has a few goodies for me in the trunk to take down Petrovich."

Scrunching her nose, she shook her head. "No. Not the car." She extended her arms and spun around. "I mean this place. These lovely automobiles."

"Oh, it's a long-term parking place where wealthy people park their cars and have them taken care of while they travel. The company stashes motorcars in places all over the world for situations like this. They're all put under the same androgynous name and it was the ID I displayed to the attendant."

"The company?"

Blake sighed. "Sorry. The CIA."

"Well, nothing says clandestine like a flashy car."

"Trust me. This is a rarity. The piece of shit we were driving earlier is more the norm."

He opened the rear passenger door, folded the back of the front passenger seat, and retrieved one of the two laptops. "Come on. Let's get a room." He showed her the laptop he recovered. "With this, we can make you a new passport."

"You're joking. You can?"

"For sure."

"What kind of passport?"

"Well, on this machine, it may limit us to only a U.S. passport, but after you get over there and this is all over, we can make you anyone you want."

She smiled at Blake and nodded her agreement.

#

Mike was in his office looking at the fresh intel his team had put together when his door opened. It was Dwight Hewins, Director of Intelligence, Cyber Division. Dwight was a tall and lengthy character. He wore gold-framed oversized eyeglasses. With his receding hairline and poofy reddish hair, Mike always said he reminded him of Bozo the Clown. "Mike, we've got a situation."

Mike turned his attention to Dwight. "What is it?"

"I think you'd better come and witness this for yourself."

They strolled back toward the control room while Dwight explained.

"Apparently Petrovich has stretched his tentacles into the government further than we thought."

They walked into the room and on the multiple screens was a wanted poster for Sofia Kuzma. Dwight pointed to the nearest monitor. "They have this posted all across the country; airports, train stations, car rental facilities, you name it."

Mike shook his head and placed his hands on his hips. "Fuck. What crime is it they say she's committed?"

"Your usual and generic 'crimes against the State'. Basic treason bullshit."

Mike chuckled and mumbled something under his breath. He strode over to another screen and read the Russian version of an All-Points Bulletin. "Well, when you're worth over a hundred billion bucks, you can buy almost anything. Okay, I'll call our asset and let him know. Thanks."

#

Blake and Sofia were in their room at the Hyatt. He had the laptop open and was working on making Sofia a new United States passport when his encrypted phone rang.

"Mackay."

"Blake. Mike. Where are you?"

"In Moscow. I have the package and am planning the extraction."

"Yeah, you'll have to hang fast for a while. Petrovich has paid someone off and the Russians put out an APB on her. We're talking full-scale search. They've got her picture plastered everywhere. You need to be extra careful now."

Blake stood and turned to Sofia. "Hold on a second." He walked into the bathroom and closed the door.

"What do they want her for?"

"Treason. And in the last three minutes, they added murder to the charges."

Blake's eyes widened at hearing the newest charge. "Murder?" He grabbed and inspected one of the hotel shampoo bottles while he listened.

"Yeah. Some sap named Nestor. I think he was the old college friend who got killed. They have her prints on a knife at his flat, where they discovered him dead. But listen, I think we've found a way for you to get close to Petrovich."

Blake tossed the tiny bottle on the counter. "How?"

"There's a conference in Tver where he is supposed to give a speech on his energy harnessing and his work on trying to control the rain. You could go to his conference and engage with him about your humanitarian profession under your David Saye alias."

Blake nodded. "Yeah, it's feasible. When is he giving his presentation?"

"Tomorrow."

"Tver is only about one hundred and fifty klicks away. I can get there in an hour. But first, I'll need to alter her appearance and retrieve the data she has."

"Excellent. In the meantime, I'll get you registered at the conference."

Blake ended the call and stepped out of the bathroom. Seated at a table by the window, Sofia gazed out at the wintry landscape beyond. As Blake exited the bathroom, she turned to him. "Is everything ok?"

Blake lied. "Yeah. Peachy."

Sofia cocked her head. "Peachy?"

He smirked. "Sorry. Yes. Everything is fine. We do have a slight change in plans."

She stepped closer. "Where—"

Blake raised his hand. "Listen. It's time for you to show me some trust. I need you to tell me where you've hidden the data."

Sofia nodded. "Yes, but I will have to go with you. You won't be able to get it without me."

"Fine, but first things first. How would you feel about a little makeover?"

17

#

Blake spent an hour altering Sofia's appearance. His skill set didn't include haircuts, but after he'd trimmed away five inches, a style started to take shape. First, he dyed her hair black, Raven Black, according to the box. After spending some time with the brush and scissors, her locks fell into a passable bob. Next, he handed her a pair of oversize sunglasses.

"Put those on and take a peek now."

She smiled. "Okay. Let's see how you did."

Turning toward the mirror, her expression was not the reaction Blake had hoped for.

Her forehead puckered and terror flashed in her eyes. "Oh, my God, it's horrible!" She pulled on a few strands on either side and then tilted her head to the right. "You couldn't even make it straight. What in the hell did you do to me?"

Reaching for the scissors, he gritted. "Here, I can straighten them."

Grabbing them from him, her tone was noticeably different. "No, you don't. Give those to me. Stay far away. You've done enough damage."

He avoided her death stare. "Hair styling wasn't part of my

training, so we'll have to live with it."

Tears welled up once again. "What's this *we'll* bullshit? Don't you mean *I'll* have to live with it?" She returned to gaze at her reflection in the mirror. "This is fucking horrible. I can't believe I trusted you. I don't even recognize myself."

Blake's jaw tightened as he went into the other room and grabbed a scarf.

"Like it or not, it was the whole point. I'd also like to emphasize 'live' being the operative word. It's better than the alternative." He tossed the scarf on the vanity as he came back in. "If you hate it so much, then put the headscarf on. It'll add to the disguise while preserving your ego."

"Huh? My ego? What the hell do you mean? I don't even understand why we are doing this. I thought we were safe now. Weren't you going to get me out of the country with the fancy new passport you made?"

"We are, but something's surfaced, and I've revised our plan."

Sofia turned back to him, removed her sunglasses, and tossed them on the scarf. "Why have they changed?" Her eyes shifted to thin slits. "What aren't you telling me?"

Blake paused a moment, admiring how her pale skin complemented her dark hair. "All right, I don't want to alarm you. Come with me."

She followed him from the bathroom, nagging him at every step. "You talked about trust. This is *my* life. I need—no, I demand you tell me what's going on. Now!"

After raising the screen to the laptop, he powered it on and chuckled. "You're in no position to demand anything. Now calm down. I said I was telling you. Be patient while I power on my computer."

Blake found the icon he needed and double-clicked it. His fingers hovered over the keyboard as he waited for the application to open. He tried to prepare her for what she was about to see.

"We've underestimated Petrovich's reach. He must have someone important in the Russian police bankrolled. We've learned there is now a nationwide search out for you. They've plastered your picture everywhere. We can't go to the airport, train stations, or even drive across the border."

"What?" Sofia leaned over and turned the laptop to face her. She scanned over the image on the screen.

She gasped. "Treason?" She continued to read. "What? Murder? They're saying I murdered Nestor!"

Tears shimmered in her eyes. She straightened and pivoted to Blake, her new, dark hair wrapped around her fingers. "But we've changed my looks. You're making me a different identification for—"

Blake shook his head. "No. It doesn't matter."

She weaved her fingers together behind her head and paced around in the bathroom.

"I don't understand! Why? Why doesn't it matter?"

Holding up his hands, he stepped toward her. "Stop. Hold on and listen to me."

Dropping her arms to her sides, she let out a deep sigh and locked eyes with him.

"Okay, fine. Now make the mouth a pinprick and the ears a trumpet. You're familiar with facial recognition software, aren't you?"

She rolled her eyes. "Of course, I'm not stupid. What's it got to do with anything?"

"All the major transportation hubs, border crossings, and so on, have it. If Petrovich can get this bulletin out on you so fast, we need to assume he has the pull power of the FSB working in his favor and they *will* be looking for you. The only way to fool this technology is to go through radical facial reconstruction surgery or find an elite Hollywood make-up artist to spend about nine hours with you. Neither of which we can do. So, for now, this is it. Deal with it."

She scoffed. "Now you're exaggerating."

"Do you honestly think I don't know what I'm talking about? This ain't my first rodeo, lady."

Sofia's brow furrowed. "Your what?"

He dismissed her with a wave. "Never mind. I know how this technology works. It's the same technology we used to catch evil guys around the globe, and I know what it takes to fool it. A quick dye and a lousy haircut won't do it."

Sofia mumbled under her breath, *"Well, at least you admit it was bad."*

"Excuse me?"

"Nothing." She pointed to the screen. "So, how was this son of a bitch able to do this? He's ruined my life!"

"Money. Lots of it. Now sit down. I need to take your photograph. After this, you're showing me where the data is. No arguments or you're on your own. Do you follow?"

Sofia nodded and turned away.

Blake reached for her chin and guided her attention back to him. "Hey! I'm not fucking around. Do you understand me?"

She swatted away his hand. "Yes!"

"Wonderful. Now relax in this chair so I can take your picture."

"Give me a moment. I'd like to wash my face and appear somewhat presentable."

After a few minutes, she came out of the bathroom and sat in the seat.

Blake aimed his phone's camera at her. "Stop pouting."

She rolled her eyes, straightened herself, and forced a smile.

Two hours later, they were in the Brabus Mercedes, weaving their way through Moscow to the destination, she told Blake. It was the Starbucks Coffee at the 5th Avenue Mall off Marshala Biruzova Street in the NW part of Moscow.

He had hoped it would be on a regular city street, surrounded by other businesses. This way, they could use the back entrance and minimize Sofia's exposure to the public. But when they drove closer, it wasn't what Blake expected. It was a five-story gray building with blue painted trim. It covered three city blocks. The Starbucks was located inside.

He dipped his chin in defeat. "Shit! Not what I was hoping for?"

"What is wrong with it? I don't understand."

He explained going in meant exposure to more people and being farther away from their car in case they needed a fast escape. Blake reached into the glove box and retrieved a set of binoculars. He used them to scan the top corners along the roof.

"As far as I can see from here, I don't spot any cameras on the roof, so that's a plus in our favor."

He then focused on the entrance door and spotted the familiar dome housing a camera. "Ah, there it is."

"What is it?"

"They've got a camera above the door. It's a domed security camera. They use them to identify any shoplifters as they leave. The best part is, I didn't locate any covering the parking lot."

Sofia glanced out the window at the car park. "What does it matter?"

Blake pulled into a parking spot well out of the camera's range. Resting his left arm on the top of the steering wheel, he pivoted toward her. "Because—if we have to get out of here fast, I don't want the vehicle appearing on security footage. The last thing we want is to show them what kind of motorcar we're in. Make sense?"

"Do you always expect danger, or are you the type of person who always causes it?"

"Ha, ha. You're funny."

Blake fought back the urge to smile. With a blank face, he turned to her. "In my line of work, there's always trouble."

There was an awkward moment of silence and they both broke out laughing.

The dark-tinted windows of the Mercedes afforded her the luxury of not having to wear the headscarf or sunglasses. As she was exiting the car, Blake grabbed them.

"Hey."

She leaned back into the car.

"Don't forget these. Go ahead and wear them."

She took the scarf and glasses and put them on as they crossed the parking lot.

Once inside the mall, Blake let her take the lead. His eyes shifted in all directions, scanning for any potential threat. They entered Starbucks. She approached the counter and recognized the girl working the register. Nestor had introduced them, and they had gone out together with a group of friends on several occasions.

The woman's palm swept across the surface of her green apron as she beamed a broad smile. "Welcome to Starbucks. Care to try a Grande Special Blend today?"

She slid her glasses to the end of her nose. "Tatiana, it's me. Sofia."

"Sofia! You look so different." Her eyes shifted to Blake. She eyed him from head to toe and smiled while she seductively curled her long, black hair around her finger. "Who's your friend?"

"He's helping me sort some things for Nestor."

Tatiana lowered her head and frowned. "I'm so sorry about him. Have the police found anything out? We're trying to assist with the funeral expenses."

She pointed to a pot on the counter. Behind it was a picture of Nestor standing next to his fish aquarium. Taped to the jar was a sign asking for donations to help with the burial costs. Sofia remembered him most in the older photo, when he still had some hair. It was just as he was when they were friends in college so many years ago.

"It's a complicated story. The police are saying I did it, but I'm being framed. I—"

Blake stepped closer and put his arm out between Sofia and Tatiana. "Okay, sorry to interrupt the reunion." He leaned into Sofia's ear and whispered a warning. "You're talking too damn much. Get what we came here for and let's go."

"Sorry." She faced Tatiana. "Nestor left something here for me. Can you please hand me my reserved cup?"

There was a collection of stainless-steel coffee cups with lids Starbucks kept for its most valued customers. Even though Sofia wasn't a regular customer, Nestor had put one aside for her. Affixed was an enormous pink "C", Russian Cyrillic for "S". Covered with rhinestones, it was flashy, pretentious, and too girly for Sofia's tastes, but it was a sweet gesture of Nestor. Tatiana placed it on the counter and Blake latched on to it.

He removed the lid, tilted the cup, and extended his hand. A USB drive slid into his palm. He popped it in his pocket. When he withdrew his hand, he had a wad of one-hundred and five-hundred-ruble bills. He stuffed them into the jar. He handed Tatiana a five-hundred-ruble bill. "We were never here."

Blake's senses kicked into top gear. The fat man pacing at the back of the counter had Nestor's old 'assistant manager' tag on his shirt, and his eavesdropping was unmistakable.

The guy disappeared into his office. After he had been inside for some time, Blake suspected something was amiss.

While Sofia continued to talk to Tatiana, he slid in behind the counter and walked toward the office. Tatiana swung her head in his direction.

"Hey, you can't go back there."

Sofia grasped her wrist. "No, it's okay."

Blake slipped through the door. The manager clutched the telephone, his eyes focused on a computer image, Sofia's picture, with WANTED in huge red letters. He lunged for the guy and grabbed the phone, hanging it up. Not wasting a nanosecond, his arm reached out and pulled the stunned man in and put him in a sleeper choke, temporarily shutting off oxygen to the brain.

"Nighty-night."

Blake kept his grasp until the man ceased to struggle and passed out.

With care, Blake rested the unconscious man on the ground and hurried out of the office.

He met eyes with Sofia.

"Come on. We've gotta go."

Sofia smiled her thanks and walked toward Blake. He grabbed her hand. They moved past a couple of tables and came to a standstill in mid-stride as two officers entered the store. Blake sized up both officials to assess the situation. The officer on the left had a wooden baton and the one on the right carried the newly assigned Vityaz PP-19-01 submachine gun. They spread out as Blake and Sofia approached.

"Stoy! Polozhite ruki za golovu."

Blake held out his palms, showing his empty hands. He raised his eyebrows and spoke slowly and deliberately.

"What did you say? I don't speak Russian." He had no intention of putting his hands behind his head.

He slowed his pace, but continued forward. A customer sat, frozen in his chair, a few steps from him.

He pleaded again. "I'm sorry. Can you tell me what you want in English?"

When the two officers glanced at each other, Blake grabbed the hot coffee sitting on the table and threw it at the officer carrying the machine gun. He lurched left toward the other officer bearing the baton. Grabbing the top of the wooden club, he pulled back and held it tight. When the policeman fought against his pull, he let go and it snapped back and struck the man's face. Blake smacked the guy in the middle of the forehead. He ripped the baton from his hands and side kicked him in the chest, knocking him to the floor.

Blake spun to his right and swung hard at the hand of the officer having the machine gun. The man screamed in pain as the sound of bones breaking filled Blake's ears.

Patrons yelled and rushed from the store, overturning chairs as they ran outside.

Blake spun left again. The first officer he hit was still down but coming around. Blake kicked the man in the head and knocked him out permanently.

He rotated back right and swiped the baton at the second cop's head. The blow sent the man back, crashing into a table and onto the floor.

Blake reached for Sofia's hand. "I told you I didn't like this. Come on!"

They ran to the car. The ferocious V-12 started with a roar. He was breathing quick to catch his breath and backed off the urge to floor it. He managed a deep sigh and exited the parking lot, slow and easy, as if nothing had happened. Sofia turned back toward the mall's entrance.

"There's nobody following us."

Blake checked his mirrors; nothing. Moments later, the sound of approaching sirens caused them both to turn toward each other; each wide-eyed with the look of *'oh crap'* on their face. Ahead on the right, two police cars turned the corner and approached them. Blake's knuckles turned white as he gripped the steering wheel. The muscles in his right leg tensed, ready to unleash the power of the supercharged engine. Both cars passed. Sofia turned around and followed the path of both police cars as Blake shifted his eyes between his mirror and the road ahead.

"They both turned into the mall."

Blake's eyes took turns between the road and concentrating on the view in the mirror. "Let's hope they stay there."

Satisfied they weren't being followed, he kept driving at a normal pace. He pulled the USB drive from his pocket. With both wrists resting on top of the steering wheel, he plugged the drive into his phone. He transferred the data from the USB drive and then opened the app to transfer it to the capsule embedded under his skin.

"Where are you putting the information?"

"Somewhere safe."

Blake scrolled through the information while it transferred, when something stood out.

"Son of a—"

"What is it?"

Blake handed her the phone. "We need to get to Tver."

18

Tver, Russia
   15:40 (12:40 GMT)
   December 20th

#

Blake and Sofia booked a room under the alias of Donald Thompson at the Park Hotel in Tver. It was nothing like the prestigious Hyatt in Moscow, but for the region, many considered it one of the better locations to stay. It was a minor boutique hotel sitting on the banks of the River Volga.

The information he'd retrieved from Sofia weighed on his mind. He'd transferred the data to Langley via a secure connection in the Mercedes. The severity of the potential consequences made for a sleepless night. Even though they shared the space, he was a gentleman and let her have the bed. Sleeping on the floor wasn't so terrible, considering some of the hellish places where he'd slept in the past.

The next morning, he got dressed while she sat on the windowsill, watching the winter wind sway the naked birch trees outside. He straightened his tie in the mirror and walked out of the bathroom.

"Do I appear presentable?"

She turned to judge his attire. He was wearing a navy-blue suit, with a double-breasted jacket. His shirt was crisp white, and the tie was yellow with tiny blue triangles.

She giggled. "Horrible. The nineties called. They want their suit back." She placed her hand over her mouth to suppress a laugh. "Is that what you're planning to wear?"

Blake's brow furrowed. He shrugged. "What?"

Removing herself from the windowsill, she approached him. "It's..." She rolled her eyes skyward as she searched for the perfect word. "Out-of-date."

"Yeah, I know. It's kind of the point." He tilted his head and smoothed out the bottom of his jacket with his hands.

"I'm supposed to be in charge of a non-profit organization out of Canada. I can't go in wearing a three-thousand-dollar suit. It wouldn't fit the part."

She puckered her lips and rubbed her chin in thought. "Hmmm, well, if you insist..." Sofia walked over to Blake and reached for the knot and loosened it. "You should at least lose the tie. It's ugly and you would draw unwanted attention to yourself by looking like you stepped in from the last century. The sport coat is awful enough."

She took a step back and inspected the jacket. "Double-breasted? Seriously?"

They laughed together.

Standing facing each other, inches apart. He took in her scent with every breath. It was floral and enticing. When she finished removing his tie, her eyes met his. They both paused. Each fraction of a second passed with aching longevity, making the moment more awkward. No longer could Blake forgo his desire. He leaned in and planted a lustful kiss on her luscious lips. There was no resistance.

Sofia pressed her body into his. The feel of her firm breasts pressing against his chest aroused him. He reached lower and urged her in the bed's direction. Her teeth gripped his bottom lip, and she pulled with a playful tug at it as she fell back onto the soft blankets. He put his knee on the bed, crawled and knelt over her. As he placed another gentle kiss on her neck, his phone rang.

"Dammit!"

He ignored it and suckled her ear lobes while she giggled. Her breath urged him for more. When the telephone sounded again, she whispered. "You had better check who's calling."

He straightened himself and sat on his knees, straddling her. He reached into his pocket, pulled out his cellphone, and glanced at it. With a heavy sigh, he got off the bed and stood. "I've gotta take this." He pointed to her. "Stay right there." He turned back toward the bathroom and answered the caller.

"MacKay."

"You're in Tver? You've got the girl?"

"Yes, boss."

"Excellent. Petrovich gives his speech in twenty minutes. If you're not at the convention, you'd better get there. Call me after you've made contact and let me know your next move."

"Wait. We've got a fresh development."

"Go ahead."

"I acquired the data and I've already sent it, so your guys should study it with care. However, I discovered something, and it has me concerned. You need to double-check it to make sure I'm right."

"Okay, what was it?"

"It was a string of numbers separated like coordinates for longitude and latitude. I think they are some of his targets."

"Good to know. I'll get them on this as soon as possible. Thanks, Bl—"

"Wait. It gets worse. I know the coordinates from when I trained with the SEALs. If I'm correct, then they are about seven miles off the coast, north of San Diego."

Mike was silent for a moment. "There's a nuclear plant there!"

"Yep. And it's right on the shoreline. Prime picking for a tsunami."

"Ok, go get this fucker and get back to me. In the meantime, I'll get the team on it and try to decipher more of the data you sent."

Blake disconnected and came back to the bedroom.

He stopped at the foot of the bed and gazed at Sofia, who lay motionless on the covers. Her luscious lips and seductive eyes invited him in.

"I have to leave now, or I'll miss this opportunity."

She frowned. "Oh, and it was getting interesting, too."

"Hold that thought. I'll be back in a few hours. We've got plenty of food here and there is water in the mini fridge. Don't open the door—"

"For anyone," they said in perfect unison.

She stood and placed her palm against his chest and kissed him on the cheek. "I know, don't worry. I'll be fine."

He paused for a moment and gathered his thoughts. Focusing on the most important thing, he set aside the near-miss with Sofia and the conversation with Mike.

"We're registered under the title of Mr. & Mrs. Donald Thompson. If you can't remember your name, glance at your passport. I'm putting the *do not disturb* sign on the door. If anyone tries to get in, I want you to use this."

He retrieved his backup pistol from around his ankle and handed it to Sofia. She sat on the edge of the bed, grasped the weapon, and inspected the back of it.

"If you're looking for a safety, it's a Glock. It has one built into the trigger. All you need to do is point and shoot. When I return, I'll knock seven times and announce myself before I come in. I won't open the door until you acknowledge. Got it?"

"Yes."

"Don't answer the door for anyone."

She playfully saluted him. "Right. Any other orders, sir?"

Blake started to say something else, but paused. He smiled.

"No."

Blake leaned over and gripped her chin with his thumb and forefinger. He kissed her once more.

"I'll be back in a couple of hours."

#

The Hotel Osnabruk was several miles to the northeast of where Blake and Sofia were staying. It also sat on the banks of the Volga River, but was more upscale and had a convention center attached to it. Blake entered the hall several minutes past the top of the hour. Petrovich addressed the crowd with his keynote speech.

Nikoli Petrovich stood confidently behind the lectern and delivered his lecture, goading like a master conductor, leading his audience through a symphony of words. They sat with rapt attention, absorbing every word of his fabricated tale.

At his rear was a huge screen displaying images of children in Sudan playing in the rain. It showed others tending flourishing vegetation in gardens on land once parched and cracked from the dry desert conditions.

While the presentation carried on, the screen came alive with vivid imagery of contented families clustered around tables, delving into the healthy bounty of homegrown vegetables.

The applause died away as the keynote speech ended and Blake eyed Petrovich as he left the stage. He pushed his way through the crowd and found the man surrounded by admirers remaining to talk to him. After waiting patiently, an opportunity presented itself. He approached and made his introduction.

"Excuse me, Mr. Petrovich."

"Yes?"

"Hello." Blake extended his hand. "My name is David Saye. I am with Canadian's Helping the World's Children. We're a non-profit based out of Vancouver, Canada."

Petrovitch smiled and nodded. "Sounds like a worthwhile organization. What can I help you with, Mr. Saye?"

"I'm intrigued by your technology. There are areas in South America we're working in, facing similar conditions. I wanted to find out some more—"

Petrovich's phone rang, and he lifted his hand. He reached into his coat pocket and dismissed the call without looking at it.

"I apologize. Please. Continue."

"No problem. I know how—"

His cellphone rang again. "I'm sorry. Allow me to silence it so we can finish talking." Petrovich's eyes narrowed when he saw the caller I. D. "I regret the interruption, but if I take this, it will only be for a moment."

Blake kept a steady eye on Petrovich as he raised the instrument to his ear, searching for any hint of emotion in the micro-expressions playing across his face and in his eyes.

"Yes." Petrovich glanced back at him, nodded and displayed an obvious forced smile. "Are you certain? Okay. I'll handle it. Congratulations on achieving something right."

He placed his phone back in his pocket and spun to face Blake.

"Mr. Saye. I must apologize. I have to return to my compound where the array is. Pressing matters on some tests we are going to be doing shortly. I would like to talk to you more, but this is urgent." Petrovich turned and walked away.

Blake's chance of getting closer to his mark was slipping away. He had to think of something, but the opportunity soon found its way back to him.

Petrovich stopped and returned to him. "Mr. Saye. Are you busy for the next couple of days?"

"I was planning to fly back to Vancouver tomorrow, but I can clear my calendar."

"Clear it then and accompany me back to the compound. You can get a full view of what it does and we can talk more."

This is perfect.

"Yes. I would like to see it. Is it far?"

Petrovich waved his hands dismissively. "A few hours in my private jet. Quick flight. We can return you to Moscow in a day or two. You'll be my guest."

"It sounds perfect. Yes. When are you leaving?"

"I'm afraid, within the hour. Are you staying here?"

"No, but I'm close. Please allow me to get my things. I can be back here in thirty minutes. Is that in order?"

Petrovich nodded, and Blake hurried out of the door.

He kept a watchful eye on Blake as he left, then walked into the next room. Vasily sat next to a laptop computer.

"You are sure he's the same man that took Sofia from the safe-house?"

Vasily spun the laptop around and pressed a key. "Yes."

When they abolished the KGB in 1991, they divided it into two divisions; the Federal Security Service and the Foreign Intelligence Service; FSB and SVR, respectively. Petrovich had people paid off in both. The laptop showed an SVR dossier, although limited, on Blake MacKay.

It had narrow information, other than he worked with the CIA and had accompanied the Navy SEALs on several previous missions. It was enough to convince him of who David Saye really was.

Petrovich leaned over and continued to read and then focused on a photo of Blake. "Well, Mr. MacKay, this makes things interesting." He straightened himself. "Vasily, excellent job—for once."

Vasily slid his chair around to face Nikoli. "Do you want me to follow him so we can get Sofia?"

"No. You've proven to be a fuck up in that area."

Vasily sighed, holding back the urge to punch his boss in the throat.

"I'm one step ahead of you."

"How so, sir?"

"I browsed through the list of attendees. Anyone who registered late, or I didn't recognize, I flagged. I had a tiny transmitter put on their conference badge. There were only three or four and Mr. Saye—or, Mr. Mackay, I should say, fell into both categories. Some would say I'm paranoid." Petrovich spun the laptop back around and pulled out his phone.

"I'd say I'm fucking brilliant." He opened an application on his phone and handed it to Vasily.

"Track him with this. After he's left, go to wherever he is and find the lovely Miss Kuzma. Drug her and bring her to the plane. Load her in the back. I don't want to give her the pleasure of riding in comfort."

Vasily took the phone. "And this MacKay? What should we do with him?"

Petrovich's jaw tightened.

"Kill him."

19

#

Blake knocked seven times and announced himself. The chain rattled as it was being unfastened. The door opened, and she welcomed him with a hug and a kiss.

Sporting the hotel's complimentary bathrobe, her damp hair was slicked back revealing her stunning cheekbones. This was the giddiest he had ever seen her in the short time they'd known each other.

She blotted her hair with a towel. "How was the convention? Did you get a chance to meet with Petrovich? Were you able to find anything out?"

Blake tried to keep his focus and not think about what was under the robe. "I can say one thing for certain. He did have his audience going."

Containing his laugh became difficult and he let it out.

Smiling, she started to giggle. "What's so funny?"

"Remember when you told me about the footage of people tending to their blossoming plants and families eating all those fresh veggies?"

She rubbed the towel on her hair, continuing to dry it. "Yes." Stopping for clarification, her eyes narrowed. "Don't tell me he played—"

"Of course he did. The same video." Blake extended his arms. "On a massive screen behind him while he was speaking." Reaching into the fridge, he pulled out a bottle of water.

"He was spewing on and on about all of these wild claims his HAARP project can do."

Rubbing her hair one final time, she walked to the window and turned back to him. "So, what did you think?"

"He's full of shit."

"I could have told you that. What about your meeting with him? Or did you not talk to him?"

"Yes, I eventually talked to him. It went okay. No. Better than expected." He hated to leave her and struggled with what to tell her. After some contemplation on what to say, he blurted it out. "I have to go."

Sofia furrowed her brow. "What? Go where? Why?"

"He's invited me to his compound to see the array. This is the perfect opportunity we need."

She tossed the damp towel on the bed. "Wait, no. It makes me feel uncomfortable. I don't trust him. And neither should you."

Blake went over to the closet, grabbed his bag, and started stuffing his gear into it. "I know. It's in my nature not to put my faith in anyone, and with Petrovich, definitely not. But this really is the best outcome I could have imagined. He's going to provide me with the most ideal position to learn all I need and hopefully shut everything down.

"How about you use your imagination on this instead?"

"What?" He raised his head. Sofia stood in front of him with her arms outstretched, holding open her robe.

Blake's gaze wandered over her body, taking in every curve, from her shapely legs and hourglass hips to her firm breasts, and at the end, settling on her captivating light green eyes. Never before had he been so punished.

Denying himself the pleasure of viewing her flawless form would be criminal. A woman who exuded both beauty and brains, whose compassionate aura made him feel elated and utterly unworthy in her presence, simultaneously.

He approached her, and with a gentle pull, pressed their bodies together. "When this is over. I promise." They kissed a hot and passionate kiss.

Blake let out a grunt. "I regret I need you to put some clothes on."

His thoughts wandered to what could have happened between them had he not gone to the convention to meet Petrovich. He shook the idea away and focused on his mission.

"This is our opportunity to get the bastard. I spoke to Marshal Reed on the way over and he is sending Sam and Oscar over to get you. They were the ones who took you to the safe house in Moscow. They know you're armed."

Sofia's lower lip puffed out and her eyes drooped like a scorned puppy. "Well, this sucks. Yeah, I remember them. You missed out."

"Believe me, I know." Blake checked the time on his phone. "They also know the procedure to knock and announce themselves."

She continued to frown. "Where are they taking me?"

"They'll take you to the Embassy in Moscow. They're working on getting you out of the country."

Blake focused on the placement of various weapons in different compartments in his bag as Sofia paced back and forth.

Her constant movement bothered him and he halted his packing. "Are you going to continue to walk backward and forwards, or are you going to tell me what's bothering you?"

She finished pacing and inserted her fingernail in her mouth and started to pick at it with her teeth. "I don't like this. You shouldn't be going there on your own. What if he knows who you are? He'll kill you."

"He doesn't know who I am and besides, I can take care of myself." Blake chambered a round into a pistol and pushed it in a hidden compartment in his bag.

"Like the agent before you? The one that disappeared?"

He stopped and straightened his shoulders. "Listen, he was young and inexperienced. He was also uninvited, so anything he did to get himself discovered or seen was automatically suspicious. His carelessness got him killed."

After zipping the pack, he set it on the floor.

"Speaking of which." He lifted the lid on his laptop and opened the 'Company's' version of Google Earth. It was much more detailed with the ability to zoom in close enough to read a matchbook.

"I need you to show me the general vicinity of where you think they shot him."

Sofia perused the satellite image of the compound and found the road exiting the main gate. She gestured to the monitor.

"Here. Before the route turns at this corner is where I stopped my car. And over here." She pointed to a cluster of trees next to an open field. She made a circle with her finger on the display. "It was in this area I heard the gunfire." She then moved the display with the mouse.

"What are you doing?"

"I want to show you something else." The map continued to move to the right. It revealed a walled village. "Here. These buildings. This is where I lived. They are furnished homes. This is where Nikoli will put you. He wouldn't want you to be in the compound."

"Let's hope you're correct. It will make it easier for me to get out and find our dead agent."

She sat up and turned to Blake. "It will *not* be easy. It is at least three or four kilometers from the main gate and there is an enormous wall around it with armed guards and security measures. Plus, it will be bitter cold there. Much colder than it is here."

He smiled. "Well, this will be an excellent test to see how useful my training is then, won't it?" He glanced at his watch.

"I've got to go. Remember, two blokes will be here in a few minutes. Get dressed."

"Wait!"

Blake stopped and turned back to meet her eyes.

"Will I see you again?"

Lying with a smile is the best he could do. "For certain."

Sofia rushed to him and wrapped her arms around him. "Thank you."

They embraced with a passionate kiss. He pulled away, gave her a wink, and walked out the door.

#

Three blocks away, Vasily and two other guys sat in their car. The application on the phone Petrovich handed him tracked his target back to this accommodation. It opened a schematic of the hotel and guided them to the location of the room. He had thrown his badge in the trash, and the software revealed he was still inside.

As his vehicle drove by, Vasily and the other two men ducked behind the safety of their dark-tinted windows, and saw him pass them by. After he had safely passed, all three of them stared at each other. The man in the back spoke first.

"Weren't we supposed to kill him?"

Vasily withdrew his pistol and chambered a round.

"We'll worry about him later. Let's get this bitch."

His henchmen, both former Russian Mafia, also loaded rounds in their H&K submachine guns.

Vasily and the other two strode along the second-floor hallway with their firearms hidden in their coats. As they proceeded, all kept a hand on standby, hovering next to their weapons. They reached Sofia's door. The Russian with a double eagle tattooed on his neck, positioned himself in front of the door. He turned to Vasily for confirmation. When he got the nod, he kicked the door in.

Sofia was kneeling, retrieving a bottle of water from the refrigerator.

"No!" In a single move, she rose and reared her arm back.

With precision, she launched the vessel at the man with the tattoo, only for it to be effortlessly swatted away by him. The other man had long hair and a horrific scar running from his left ear, across his face, through his lips and ending at his chin. He dashed in behind and wrapped his arms around her.

"No! Get away!" She wiggled her body, trying to escape.

The assailant with the double eagle tattoos positioned himself in front of her. She waited until he was closer, kicked out and slammed him in the chest. He grunted and rushed back toward her. He punched her square in the face. Her head snapped back. Blood gushed from her nose.

Sofia smirked. "You hit like a girl!"

He drew back his arm, but Vasily grabbed it and stopped him from delivering the punch.

The head thug pulled his man back and stepped forward. "Miss Kuzma, do not think we won't beat you to a pulp. It is up to you, but either way, you're coming with us."

A metallic taste filled her mouth as the blood seeped past her lips.

Her face contorted and with a gaze oozing with disgust and malice, she screamed, "Go to hell!"

She spat at Vasily. He closed his eyes as the crimson saliva spread over his face, then backhanded her across the cheek. He reached for her shirt, pulled her close, and wiped the spit off his face.

"You've chosen the hard way."

He nodded to the scar-faced henchman. His grip loosened. There was a sharp prick on the side of her neck, then darkness.

\#

Oscar and Sam did a quick sweep of the outside for anything suspicious. They entered the hotel and proceeded to Sofia's floor.

Sam held the stairwell door open for his companion. "Have they made the arrangements to get this woman out of the country yet?"

"I don't know. All I know is we're supposed to bring her back to the embassy. Marshal said he was taking care of it."

Oscar was in the lead as they trotted up the stairs. When they got to the door, he pushed it open for Sam and he went onto the level. "Don't forget to knock seven times and announce ourselves. I'd hate to get shot."

Sam chuckled. "Yeah, MacKay said she was kind of trigger-happy."

As Sam rounded the corner, three men left a room. One with long hair had a woman draped over his shoulder.

Sam withdrew and pointed his pistol along the hall. "Stop! Don't take another step!"

Vasily turned back toward Sam and lifted his weapon. The man with the tattoo flung his overcoat back, raised his MP5 and opened fire.

Training and muscle memory kicked in and Sam dropped flat.

"Gun!"

Bullets penetrated the wall where Sam had been standing a fraction of a second earlier. Oscar ducked and rounded the corner. A bullet tore through his left shoulder. He hit the floor.

"Aughh! Shit! I'm hit, I'm hit!" He reached for his shoulder.

Sam let off a shot in the direction of the men but aimed for the ceiling instead, using the round as a warning. He couldn't take the chance of hitting Sofia. They all vanished through the other fire exit door.

After they were gone, he spun around. "Oscar! You ok?"

"Fuck! Yeah, I'll be all right. I think it went clean through."

Sam tugged out a handkerchief, folded it, and applied pressure to the wound. "Here, keep applying pressure." He reached out his hand and pulled Oscar to his feet.

"We've gotta go."

The two agents barreled down the stairwell and exited into the parking lot. The sound of high revs of a vehicle approaching filled their ears as they raced to their car.

A black Mercedes sped toward them.

Sam's eyes widened in surprise. "Lookout!"

Oscar swiftly rushed to the opposite side of the motorcar while bullets mercilessly tore through the side of their blue Chrysler 300. Climbing into the back seat, he frantically searched for the first aid kit as his partner skillfully maneuvered the vehicle. Determined, they chased after the woman they were supposed to protect, relentlessly tearing through quiet residential streets and narrowly avoiding collisions. Eyes focused ahead, he gunned the engine and positioned themselves right behind them. He rammed into the back bumper. The Benz lurched before the tires regained their grip and sped forward.

The power of the V-8 once again allowed them to get close. Sam tried to edge the vehicle to the back quarter panel to perform a pit maneuver, only to be met with a barrage of gunfire that shattered the front windshield.

Protected in the back seat, Oscar released the pressure from his wound. "Motherfuckers! Go get their ass!"

Sam floored it and slammed into the back of the Merc again.

"Be careful! If you make them crash and it kills the woman; it's your ass!"

"Well, what the hell do you want me to do?"

The Mercedes abruptly turned into a residential neighborhood, causing a collision with another vehicle, temporarily blocking their path. Eyes wide and hyper-focused on the road, he turned the wheel hard and narrowly missed the impediment.

"Finally, I got the bleeding to stop."

He inserted a fresh magazine into his pistol.

"You're all good now?"

"Yeah. Try to get close to it again. I'll shoot out its tires."

Tires screeched at the Benz skidded around the next corner. It made a series of direction changes over the next several blocks. The screeching of tires and roaring of engines reverberated through their eardrums as they pressed on, protesting against the tarmac.

A red Volga pulled out from where the kidnappers had last slid around. It blocked their path. Sam slammed on his brakes and honked his horn.

"Fucking move!"

The driver gestured and backed out of the way. He gunned the motor and followed. Brake lights illuminated in front of him.

"Ah ha! We've got the bastards. Dead end." He pushed the parking brake and slid the car sideways to block the exit.

Reverse lights illuminated, and the engine wailed. It approached them at increasing speed.

"Oh shit! They're going to ram us! Hold on!"

The heavier German vehicle slammed into the driver's rear side quarter panel. It spun them around and rendered them immobile. As the back window shattered, the Mercedes continued its escape in reverse. It did a one-eighty and sped off.

The V-8 struggled to come alive. "Come on!"

It continued to give him grief.

Oscar was careful while brushing off shards of glass. "Hurry! They're getting away!"

"I'm trying!" He pushed the ignition button again. Nothing. He slapped the dash with the palm of his hand.

"Start god dammit!"

It finally roared to life.

"HA!"

They continued their pursuit. Both rear tires screeched and released a plume of white smoke.

They reached the end of the block and sped off after Sofia and the three men.

Oscar pointed. "There! It's the M10. It heads toward the airport. That's gotta be where they went."

"Yep! I'm sure I saw those assholes heading that way."

They sped up the ramp and onto the highway. He leaned on the gas pedal and careened through traffic like a wild bull attempting to catch them. "Do you see them?"

"Not yet. Keep going."

They dodged and weaved until they approached a slow-moving commuter in the passing lane. He honked the horn.

"Get the fuck outta the way!"

He flashed his lights, but the vehicle wouldn't move.

"Fuck it!"

He veered off to the left shoulder. Horns wailed as he sped by, kicking up dust and gravel from the medium. After five more minutes, the black sedan came into Sam's view.

"There. Past the yellow van." He pushed the 300's engine to its limit.

Oscar checked the bandage on his wound. "How far to the airport?"

"At this rate, not long."

Sam glanced in his rearview mirror.

"Oh-oh. We've got company."

Oscar turned around. A police car was approaching with its lights flashing and the sound of its siren now within his ears' range.

Sam caught Oscar's eyes in the mirror. "Do what you've gotta do."

He weaved over two lanes of traffic. The police followed. Continuing to change lanes, Oscar waited for a decent shot. Positioning his weapon out of the open side window, he emptied his magazine into the front right fender and punctured the tire.

As it deflated, the wheel cut into the rubber. The disintegration of the tire made the vehicle unstable. It lost control, flipped and rolled multiple times along the middle of the highway.

All lanes of traffic behind them came to a grinding halt. Commuters swerved and hit each other, trying to avoid the carnage of the pursuing police as it rolled to a stop on its roof.

"Ooo, that's gonna leave a mark." He turned to face forward. His eyes met Sam's in the rearview mirror.

"Meh. He'll be okay."

They both chuckled.

Oscar pointed. "There! It's getting off."

The Mercedes roared off the freeway and bolted toward the exclusive airfield, catering only to private aircraft.

He veered off the M10 and trailed them onto the airport grounds, steering toward the cluster of hangars. In the blink of an eye, the Benz darted through a nearby parking lot, vanishing into the entrance of a cavernous structure.

Oscar gestured. "That's the direction they went. Let's go after them."

A small security gate with one sentry was the only thing stopping them. Increasing speed, the lone guard dove out of the way as the Chrysler broke through the barricade's arm. He continued following the other car's path and entered through the massive expanse.

They didn't notice the dozen men standing poised on either side of the second level, weapons at the ready. Without warning, they unleashed a barrage of gunfire, their lethal bullets tearing through the thin metal shell of the 300.

Flying lead penetrated the cabin and tore through the bodies of both agents. The car swerved left and slammed into a steel beam on the far side of the building and came to a stop.

A small fire started under the vehicle. One man raced to it and extinguished the blaze while another capped off one final round into each of the agents' heads.

The Mercedes continued out onto the tarmac to the private jet, standing half a kilometer away. It approached it from the rear, out of sight from anyone inside the cabin.

#

Blake sat on the plane as Petrovich talked to him about the weather array. He had a genuine interest in how it was supposed to work and hoped to learn some clues on how to shut it down.

He glanced out of the window. "We've been sitting here for some time. Are we waiting for someone?"

Petrovich stood at the lavish mahogany and granite bar. "I'm sure you can understand Russians having an affinity for fine vodka, yes?" He raised a bottle and smiled.

Blake returned the smile. "Of course."

"Being in the middle of Siberia, one cannot run out and get a fresh supply. I will take back three or four cases with me when I can. I also get several more of wine."

One of Petrovich's men came onto the plane and nodded to him.

"And apparently it is here. Now, as soon as they load it below, we can go."

#

They had given Sofia seventy-five micrograms of fentanyl back at the hotel to knock her out. The man with the long hair dumped her in the cargo hold. He tied and gagged her in the unlikely event the drugs wore off before the trip ended.

#

The familiar sound of a belly door closing filled the cabin. Moments later, Vasily walked onto the plane. He stopped when he noticed Blake.

"I—I see we have an additional passenger."

Petrovich turned to face him. His gaze cut through him like a fine Japanese blade. "Yes, we do."

He stepped toward Blake and handed him a glass of chilled vodka.

"Allow me to introduce to you, Mr. David Saye, from Canada." He turned to his guest. "This is my assistant, Vasily."

Oh shit! Does he recognize me?

He raised his drink. The man nodded.

I guess not. So, you're the son of a bitch that's been causing so much turmoil. I sure would love to throw you off this plane.

"Now we are ready to go. Sit back and relax. We'll be there in a couple of hours."

20

Petrovich's Research Facility
   Eastern Siberia, Russia
   02:45 (18:45 Dec. 20th GMT)
   December 21st

#

Blake was in his assigned quarters, and just as Sofia had told him, it was in the small hamlet a few kilometers away from the central compound.

His winter gear was all white, with heated thermal underwear powered by a thin lithium battery sewn into the fabric. It was minus fifteen degrees Celsius outside, unusually mild for the season. Earlier, he'd spent the evening walking around the residential village.

The guards understood he was an invited guest and let him have free rein. To anyone he met, he introduced himself as his alias, David Saye. He spoke with several residents and a few sentries, making small talk, all the while gathering as much intelligence as he could.

Any person who has ever worked in the business of clandestine affairs will attest, never assume you are safe. As he toured the area, he was careful to ask the correct questions in the proper manner to gather information. He didn't want to raise any suspicions.

He had a hunch Petrovich knew who his real identity was. If his network was as vast and deep as Blake suspected, it was almost a certainty. If Vasily knew, he didn't give any indication on the plane.

Of course, he could have waited until they landed to tell his boss once he was out of sight. Regardless, there was nothing he could do about it now. He would operate under the assumption he knew, but play it out as if he didn't. His primary mission now was to find Lance Tucker. Everything else was secondary.

With a fresh blanket of snow and Christmas lights strewn throughout, long icicles hung from the eaves, like icing on a gingerbread house. It resembled something out of a Dickens novel; though one with a sinister twist.

Sofia was correct when describing the village as walled with security, but as luck would have it, it wasn't as secure as she let on. There was an armed guard at the only gate. A few guards patrolled inside the walls at regular intervals. There were oscillating CCTV cameras, mounted along the top of the stone wall, monitored at a central hub.

The residential area covered twenty acres and was a working small town in the middle of Siberia. It included a variety of amenities, such as a grocery, restaurants, and a general store stocked with everything from clothing to appliances. The site even boasted a decent-sized theater, which was used for plays, concerts, and recent Hollywood movie screenings.

In speaking to the residents, he found out all the businesses received new stock and supplies once a week. They arrived by planes, landed at the private airstrip, and trucked to a warehouse, and tonight was a night for deliveries.

The box truck delivering the food stopped in the village before it continued to the central compound. This would be his ride to the spot where the remains of Agent Tucker would be.

He checked his watch. The delivery vehicle would be here soon, unloading fresh stocks. He opened the smartphone app Alice installed to locate the body of the late operative. A tiny circle spun as the screen read:

"Searching...".

Blake mumbled under his breath. "Come on. Find it."

Alice mentioned the microscopic power cell in the capsule was going to be exceptionally low, if not dead. Placing the cellphone on the side table in his quarters, he went to his bag. He removed the silencer for his Glock. His phone 'beeped' as he screwed the piece to the end of his barrel. He walked over, lifted it, and eyed a small red dot on the map.

It displayed a message. *Warning—Transmitter battery level extremely low. <1%.*

"Shit! Okay, Agent Tucker. You'd better have something exciting for me."

Hacking into the CCTV camera system was easy. Blake learned early during his MIT days, the vast majority of administrators do not alter the default configurations for entry. Even though there are multiple systems, there are only a few manufacturers.

Blake entered the typical standard usernames and passwords. On the fourth try, using Username: admin, Password: 1111, he had full control of the entire setup. Not only could he see what the cameras captured on his phone, but he could also regulate them. Testing it out, he rotated the camera in front of the theater 180 degrees and back.

To start, he found the one that watched his residence and diverted it to point the opposite way. Upon leaving, he avoided the surveillance and the few guards patrolling the area. Blake made his way to the center of the village. He could hear the idling diesel engine on the next block.

Standing with his back against the wall of the grocery store, careful not to be seen, he peeked around the corner. There was one individual in the doorway with a clipboard, and there was another person in the vehicle loading packages. A gust of wind blew and the guy with the clipboard rocked back and forth.

"Hurry it up. It's cold out here."

The other man descended the ramp with a hand trolley full of packages. "You're such a wimp. Instead of complaining, why don't you come in and help me unload these boxes?"

When both men were inside, Blake scanned the area for guards. He glanced at his phone and could see the vehicle through a camera's eyes. Taking control of the camera, he made it pan away in the opposite direction. Quickly, he ran over and rolled underneath the truck as soon as it was out of the camera's view. Attached to his garment was a white webbing strap with a carabiner clipped to the front. He pulled himself to the underbelly of the vehicle and clipped the carabiner to the truck's frame. Finding a good foothold, he tightened his belt and held on.

Fifteen minutes later, the driver finished unloading the supplies and put the truck in gear. It left the village and headed north, toward the central compound. With care not to drop it, he removed his cellphone from his pocket. He could see the signal for Agent Tucker's location was still present on his phone.

Come on battery. Hold on for a little longer.

The wind blew under the lorry, and even with his thermal outfit, the cold seeped into him. After two kilometers, he came within half a klick of the signal. He unclipped the carabiner. The vehicle ascended an icy incline. Its speed had slowed to about thirty kilometers per hour.

Blake dropped to the roadway and slid a couple of meters on the ice. He let the truck pass and then rolled over to the side of the road. The tree line was fifty meters away. But first, he had to climb a small mountain of snow created by the snowplows' constant clearing of the route.

Blake climbed to the top of the frozen mound, blackened by the sand and filth sprayed from the thoroughfare. Before reaching the bottom, he stopped and found a suitable place to sit. He removed two foldable snowshoes made of carbon fiber from his backpack. He unfolded them and fitted them. Next, he pulled out a collapsible shaft and assembled it.

He used the three-meter pole to steady himself as he descended the remaining distance of the freezing pile. He stuck the post into the snow and stepped down. The width of the shoes distributed his weight, but he still sank a few centimeters. Inserting the rod, it sunk two meters in the fluffy snow before it found frozen ground.

Under the thick pine canopy, the snow wasn't as deep. The tops of the trees blocked a lot of the snow from reaching the ground. He peered at his phone again and headed toward the signal. It was only one hundred meters away.

As he trudged through the woods, an owl made its presence known, and the wind whistled through the pine needles. He could hear the faint hum of power emanating from the central compound in the distance. The lights illuminated the low-hanging clouds over the horizon.

Blake was only twenty-five meters away when he glanced one more time at his phone. The screen had a spinning circle again. *'Searching...'*

Son of a bitch! Are you kidding me?

The capsule's battery was dead, and the indicator was gone, but he knew Lance's corpse was nearby.

He continued to the location where the signal had come from. When he got to the region where he assumed Agent Tucker's cadaver would be, there was nothing but a fresh blanket of snow.

Dammit! I've got to be close.

Growing up in Colorado and being an avid skier, he had mastered mountain rescue techniques. He paced the area in a grid pattern and jabbed the pole into the snow. He sought as rescuers of avalanche victims did, feeling shallow parts could be a body. As he searched, he understood how to feel the difference between the ground and a rock or downed tree.

Ten minutes passed, and he'd covered eighty percent of the zone. Four meters in front of him, there was something dark protruding from the snowfall. He trudged over and inspected it. It was a portion of the fiberglass body of a snowmobile.

Okay, I'm in the right area.

He continued and poked around in the snow when he stopped for a moment. A massive pine tree loomed before him, its bark shorn away, and its trunk pockmarked by bullet holes.

That's interesting.

Blake headed for the tree and searched near the base. On the opposite side, four meters from where he found the snowmobile part, he discovered what he was searching for. The sound it made and the way the shaft reacted in his hand were unmistakable.

He dropped to his knees and started pushing away the snow.

A half meter below the surface, he found agent Lance Tucker. The cold had prevented any decomposition and the fresh snowfall had masked any scent. Blake identified the damage around Lance's neck as dog bites and the bullet hole in his head was obvious.

Blake hurried and cut away Agent Tucker's sleeve. He inspected the body's arm for the location of the capsule. Once he located it, he used his knife to extract it.

Gotcha. Let's see what other goodies you still have on you.

Blake searched Lance's pockets and uncovered his phone. No surprise, it was dead. He turned him over and went through the rest of his clothes. He pulled out a stack of flat, explosive patches. On their own, they can be dangerous; enough to kill a man if placed in the right place.

However, their primary purpose was to act as a catalyst for larger explosions. Sticking them to a fuel tank, they would be the igniter and the fuel tank, the weapon. They detonated remotely with a signal from either a phone or a proprietary device.

"Well, these could be useful."

Blake stuffed them into his pockets, along with the phone and capsule.

After fishing through the rest of Lance's pockets, he stood and surveyed the surrounding area. No sign of anything or anyone. He turned back to Lance.

"Sorry buddy, but I've got to leave you here. We'll come back and get you when this is all over."

Blake started his long walk back to the village.

#

He arrived back at his quarters with no incidents. He tracked the cameras on the outside of the village and made it over the wall without being detected. His only concern was if a guard patrolled the outer wall and saw his tracks in the snow.

Blake dragged a pine branch behind him to mask his tracks and, on camera, the flat light hid the tracks. He didn't believe they patrolled outside the wall in person, and he hadn't witnessed any footprints or vehicle tracks to make him think otherwise.

Blake took Lance's phone, plugged it in, and let it charge. While he waited, he fixed a hot cup of tea, hoping it would help to warm his body.

After a few minutes, he powered on the phone. He opened the app used to detonate the small explosives. A screen appeared and revealed where Agent Tucker had already placed and set two of the devices.

Well, well. Aren't you ingenious?

Lance had placed the devices on two of the gas mains sitting outside of the property wall. The force of the explosion would propel it underground into every nook and cranny of the building, triggering blasts everywhere.

It appears as if you've done a goodly portion of my work for me. Thank you.

Blake removed the capsule from his pocket and put it into a specially crafted USB drive and plugged it into his computer. The screen opened with a window of various files. He read them and reviewed the intel. The information detailed a full schematic of the compound and its vulnerable points. It also revealed what Blake had suspected; future targets and the dates and times they were to be hit.

The nuclear power plant north of San Diego was, in fact, the next target. Blake saw the date.

"Oh, shit!"

21

Petrovich Research Facility
    Eastern Siberia, Russia
    10:30 (02:30 GMT)
    December 22nd

#

The slap across her face brought Sofia one step closer to the realm of consciousness. "Wake up!"

The tormenting voice broke into her haze and physical pain. The trickle of something wet tickled her lips. She needed to rest. Her head rolled to the side.

Did someone touch me? Whoever you are, leave me alone. Let me sleep. Wait, am I dreaming?

Her eyelids flickered and then moved enough to make out the fuzzy silhouette of Petrovich, and to his rear, Vasily stood guard. There were two more light slaps on her cheek. "Come on, rise and shine, lovely lady. Wake up."

The arid winter air had left her throat bone dry. With the intention of bringing her hands to her mouth, Sofia soon realized they were tightly bound behind her back. The sobering realization of the situation forced her eyes to pop open as her heart pounded faster. "What the— where is this place?" As she spoke, her voice cracked, and the once commanding demand withered into a pitiful whine.

A smug Petrovich stood before her and outstretched his arms.

"Gaze around you."

His cocky grin exuded such arrogance. It made Sofia's skin crawl. She turned her head from side to side and recognized the inside of Petrovich's office. "You son of a bitch! What am I doing here?"

Anger thundered through him. His eyes narrowed and his jaw clenched. "Shut up!"

He backhanded her across the face and circled around her with slow and deliberate steps. "You've been a busy little cow, haven't you?"

Sofia said nothing but stared with condemning eyes, following him, until he was out of her sight. Petrovich snapped his fingers, and Vasily handed him a bottle of water. He opened it and stood behind her. Reaching for her hair, he pulled back and leaned over her face. "You would like some of this, no?"

Cracks lined her lips, while her throat burned with thirst. Despite her desperation for a drink, she refused to show weakness and give him satisfaction. "Fuck you!"

His eyes narrowed once again. She could hear him gritting his teeth. "Fine. You contemptuous whore." He squeezed the bottle and forced the liquid out over Sofia's face. He released her hair and walked around to confront her.

"You don't need to say anything." He leveled a pointed finger directly at her, a silent accusation hanging in the charged air between them. "I know the data you took, and I discovered who you handed it to. Our guest, Mr. Saye—or should I say, Mr. Mackay?"

Petrovich paused, his eyes narrowing into a menacing glare as his gaze locked onto Sofia. Even as her head reeled, she faced her captor, pulling her wrists against the straps. He smirked. "Yes—I know who he is. He'll be here in a moment and will be joining you. You've both caused me a lot of problems, but rest assured, it won't be the case any longer."

"What are you going to do?" Her voice still cracked, failing to exert the anger boiling inside her.

"Oh, so she speaks?"

Petrovich leaned over within an inch of her face. "You're so smart— you figure it out."

#

Blake was ready for his meeting with Petrovich and waited for his ride to take him to the compound from his quarters. He called Mike from his secure satellite phone, and as usual, he answered after the first ring.

"Where are you?"

"The residential area of Petrovich's research headquarters. I located our missing asset."

"And?"

"Dead."

"Too bad, but we suspected it. What else?"

"I recovered the capsule and pulled the information from it. It had a layout of the compound plus a significant amount of other intelligence. Our guy did a first class job and had already planted several catalysts to start a chain reaction. They're still where he deposited them, and they're armed. Part of me wants to set them off now and make a clean getaway, but I think I must add a few more inside."

"Fantastic work. However, what I have to tell you is going to make you rethink your plans."

Blake's eyes narrowed, and he stepped over to the window to check if his ride had arrived. "How so?"

"We need to assume they got the woman."

"What? Do you mean Sofia? What the fuck happened?"

Blake turned around and went over to the table. He grabbed his pistol, chambered a round, and tucked it into the small of his back.

"The two men you sent to get her never reported back to the Embassy. Reed hasn't heard from them, and their phones don't appear on GPS. They're presumed dead."

Blake stood still for a moment. He had a flashback to waiting on the tarmac for such a long time.

It popped into his brain like a vivid burst of lightning. It was Sofia they brought onboard, not booze. "The crates."

"What?"

"Uh, Petrovich. He mentioned he liked vodka—I flew here with him. We waited for what he claimed were cases of vodka being loaded on the aircraft—it was Sofia."

"So, he knows who you are."

"Yeah. I figured he did. His fat ass henchman, Vasily, was on the flight too."

"Rethinking your plans?"

He stood and stared out the window and over the wall, his mind cranked through all the possibilities. A lone fawn walked through the woods just inside the tree line.

Just one deer? There must be more nearby.

"Blake?"

"What?"

"I said, are you reconsidering your strategies?"

"No. But I am weighing my options. I'm still going in."

A car stopped in front of his quarters. "They're here. Gotta run." Without waiting for a response, he disconnected the call.

#

Blake scrutinized the entrance before passing through the door. He tucked a notebook under his arm and stuck a pen in his pocket. He resembled any other visitor. The room was typical of a reception place for any company, a waiting room, public restrooms, various fake plants in the corners, and a small sitting space.

He'd put the stack of explosive patches in one of his outer jacket pockets and Agent Tucker's cell phone in his back pocket. Someone in a white lab coat greeted him. Blake guessed him to be approximately fifty years old, with sandy brown hair combed over to cover his obvious balding. "Mr. Saye, welcome to the array. My name is Pitor. Mr. Petrovich has asked me to show you around before meeting with him."

They shook hands. "Sounds good."

Pitor waved him in. "Follow me."

They entered through a set of double doors leading to a lengthy ramp down to the main level. The floor was gray concrete, and the walls were cinderblock, painted blue. There was a long white stripe, half a meter broad, on the wall about two meters from the bottom, and it followed the angle of the ramp as they walked.

"We're headed underground. All the radio antennae will be over us at ground level."

As they strode into the vast subterranean area, over their heads were huge electrical boxes around one-meter square. They spaced them about three meters apart on the ceiling. Blake pointed to them. "What are those?"

"Those are the power grids for each of the array antenna. We transmit power to them, which they collect and store, much like a battery. They then release it to the antenna above in controlled and precisely timed pulses."

As they walked, Blake scanned the area and made a mental

checklist: pipes, conduit used for electrical and gas. His eyes followed a pipe along the ceiling labeled for gas until it descended and went along the wall. He pulled a single patch from his pocket and sauntered over to the pipe. He directed Pitor's attention away from him. "What's the glass-walled room in the middle?"

When his escort turned his head, he placed a patch on the back of one of the gas pipes. "Good question, Mr. Saye. It is the central control room. It's where we regulate the power sent to the antenna."

They continued to walk in the vast room and Blake attached about a half dozen more patches to gas pipes without his guide knowing. Pitor's cellphone rang. "Yes. Of course, right away." Blake's companion ended the call and put his phone away. "Mr. Petrovich is ready for you now."

They walked for at least ten minutes before the landscape changed from industrial gray and blue to more lavish and opulent surroundings. "Through these doors is Mr. Petrovich's outer office. We'll go in there and you can wait for him. Would you like any coffee or water while you are waiting?"

"No, thanks."

Pitor opened the door and extended his arm. His gaze affixed on Blake as he entered the room. Two bodies lunged from either side and grabbed Blake. His reflexes kicked in and shook loose the two guys trying to hold him. He spun to his immediate right and punched the first man in the face.

Out of his peripheral vision, he counted over two men. As he turned to the left, the man behind him hit him in the back of the head with the butt of his rifle. Blake was lying prone on the floor, as a sharp prick in his neck sent him and the world around him into total darkness.

#

Blake's stomach reeled from the punch delivered by Vasily. He shook his head. The torpidity of the drug they injected hung over him like a drunken stupor. The backhand across his face brought him more out of the dark. Tied to a wooden chair, his hands were secured behind his back. When he could finally focus, Petrovich was in front of him, holding his pistol and cell phone in one hand, rocking them back and forth with his wrist. "Looking for these, Mr. Saye—or is it MacKay? I don't know which."

Sofia cried out. "Blake!"

Blake pivoted to his right. Sofia sat bound to a chair like him. He turned his attention back to Petrovich. "You know who I am."

"Yes, of course I do, and I know why you're here. But now we have you, and there isn't a damn thing you can do."

"It wasn't a question. I assumed you knew. And as for me, not doing anything. We'll see about that."

Petrovich laughed in arrogant confidence. "Mr. MacKay, you've run out of time. You see—because you are here now—I'm not only going to move up the timetable of my next attack, but I've even expanded it."

The bad feeling hit his gut. He was afraid to ask, but had to. "What do you mean?"

"Not only am I going to target the Pacific, but also the Eastern seaboard and the Gulf of Mexico. I have placed billions of dollars in puts on hundreds of companies. The devastation will affect all of them."

Petrovich let the impact of his words sink in. He took two steps back so he could see both of his prisoners. "I'll walk away with half a trillion dollars." He pointed to Blake. "And I'll send the United States into an economic tailspin. All thanks to you, I might add."

"You son of a bitch!" Blake tried to shake loose of his restraints. Vasily stepped forward and delivered a hard left to Blake's jaw and knocked him over.

Sofia shouted. "You bastard! Stop it!"

Petrovich nodded to Vasily to right Blake's chair. As he did, Blake reached behind him in his pocket. Agent Tucker's phone was still there. Vasily righted the chair and slapped Blake in the face again. Piercing eyes and a clenched jaw greeted Vasily when he glanced back at Blake.

"I'm gonna kick your ass."

Vasily smiled and leaned in. "Sure you are." He turned and walked back behind Petrovich.

"You won't get away with this." Blake spat blood on the floor.

Petrovich smirked. "You know—Agent Tucker said the same thing. Right before I put a bullet through his brain."

Vasily and the other men in the room laughed. Petrovich chortled along.

"Well, I have a feeling Agent Tucker hasn't finished with you yet."

"You idiot Americans and your stupid sayings. I don't even know what it means."

Blake slipped his tied hands into his pocket behind him.

"Well, perhaps this will help you understand." Blake pressed a button on the phone to detonate the charges. Explosions ripped through the halls. The shock of the detonations shook the structure. People screamed out beyond the doors. Petrovich glared at Blake with burning intensity. "What have you done?"

A voice from outside the office yelled, "Mr. Petrovich! Come quick!"

Petrovich turned toward the door, then back to Vasily. He jerked a thumb at Blake. "Keep them here! If they try anything, kill them both!"

Another explosion jolted the building. Fire blasted out of the fireplace. Vasily pivoted to look. Blake seized the opportunity and stood. It was foolish they didn't bind his legs. He spun around and rushed at Vasily. The legs of the chair pointed at his target. He rammed the bald Russian and pushed hard toward the wall.

Vasily and the chair slammed against the wall. The wooden chair cracked. Blake pushed forward and then back. He bashed Vasily into the wall again. The chair cracked further. Still tied, he swung his midsection and hit his target across the groin with as much force as he could muster.

The chair splintered apart, and Vasily grunted and winced in pain as he slid to the ground. Like skipping rope, Blake jumped and forced his hands from behind his back, under his feet, and to his front. He reached for one of the chair legs. He grabbed it and swung hard at Vasily, who held up his left arm in defense. "No!"

"Fuck you, asshole!"

Blake kicked him in the gut. When Vasily lowered his arm to block more kicks, Blake connected with Vasily's forehead and knocked him out cold. He ran behind Sofia and unfastened her wrists. "I'm sorry. I didn't know they had you until right before I got here."

After being freed, she stood and wrapped her arms around him. He smiled. "Thanks, but we have to get out of here." He held out his bound hands, and she untied them. Alarms were blaring. It was complete chaos. Her breathing quickened with fear of the unknown. "What did you do?"

"I set small charges on the gas lines. This whole place is ablaze."

Sofia shook her head. "No, we have to do more. We must destroy the antenna. This fire is below them. If they put the blaze out, the antenna will still be functional."

"What else can we do? Do you know something we can do to

destroy them?"

"Yes. I can send a power spike through them and fry the electronics."

"Can you do it from here?"

"No. The central control room. It's—"

"I know where it's at." Blake grabbed her hand, and they ran out of Petrovich's office into the main underground area. It was chaotic. People scattered to escape. Others tried to help extinguish the various fires. Someone approached them in a golf cart. It was Pitor. Blake waved at him and as he slowed, he reached in, pulled him from the driver's seat and slammed his head against a concrete support column. The man collapsed to the ground. "Get in!"

#

Petrovich was less than one hundred meters away. "Put those flames out!"

He reached out and grabbed an individual who was barreling for the exit. "Where the fuck do you think you're going?"

Rivulets of sweat streamed down the man's face as he stared out with wide, saucer-like eyes. 'This place is gonna blow!' His voice trembled with urgency. "We have little time. We need to leave - now!"

Petrovich grasped the guy's collar. Another explosion erupted. They both ducked. "Get your ass back and help with this fire!"

The man shook his head. "You can go to hell!" He brushed away Nikoli's grip.

With wild eyes, Petrovich reached out and reclaimed his hold and screamed at him. "You're useless to me! You will die!"

Petrovich pushed the man back, lifted his pistol and shot him in the face. Others raced toward Petrovich. He raised his pistol and fired into the ceiling. The ricochet hit someone in the leg. The guy fell to the floor and shrieked. Everyone stopped. "Get back and fight this fire or I'll slaughter you all!"

They scattered and ran to find another exit. As Petrovich scanned the area through the chaos, Blake and Sofia got in the golf cart. He opened out his arms. "Vasily! You've failed me again! I will kill you next!" He sprinted after them.

#

Nobody was present in the abandoned central control room when Blake and Sofia arrived. Inside were banks of computer screens and keyboards lining all the walls. Blake drew his pistol and peered outside the door. "Do what you've gotta do, but make it quick."

Sofia pulled up a chair and started typing on a keyboard. Blake glanced at her. "How much longer?"

"Be patient. I just sat down." She continued to type as he stood watch. After another minute, he lost his patience and hustled over to her. She was still tapping the keys. "What's taking so long?"

"I'm starting the flow of power to those silver boxes hanging from the ceiling. Above all of them are the—"

"Yeah, I know, the antenna. What's next?"

"Those control the frequency of pulse bursts. During normal operation, the bursts are between two and three seconds apart. I can't transmit multiple bursts together, so I have to reprogram them to send them microseconds apart. Doing so should fry all their circuits. I only need another minute or two."

"Make it thirty seconds." Blake dashed back over to the door when Petrovich burst in, weapon in hand. Blake seized his arm and struggled to strip it away. The pistol fired, and a bullet tore through the monitor next to Sofia. She screamed. He wrestled Petrovich to the ground and slammed his wrist against the floor until the gun fell out.

Petrovich flailed wildly and clocked Blake on the side of his head. Blake rolled over and Petrovich dove for his weapon. He lunged at Petrovich and grabbed him around the waist. With Petrovich lying on top of him, he rolled over onto his back and put Petrovitch in a chokehold.

Sofia's gaze remained fixed on the screen. "I'm almost there!"

An explosion from outside the control room shattered two windows to her right. Glass flew everywhere. "Hurry the hell up!" Blake punched his adversary in the head.

Sofia raised her hands. "I got it!"

Blake struggled to keep his foe contained. "Do it!"

She pressed the enter key. In an instant. sparks emanated from all the boxes in the ceiling. More fires broke out. Petrovich elbowed Blake in the stomach twice and freed himself. He stood and yelled, "You're all going to fucking die, anyway."

He turned and rushed out of the control room, jumped in their cart, and sped away. Blake grabbed her hand and pulled her. "Come on!"

As the two exited the room, bullets whizzed past their head and shattered the glass behind them. "Shit!" Three men were coming at them. He grasped both hands around her waist and pushed her back in the direction of the room. "Duck! Back inside."

Sofia ducked and screamed. "The fire! It's getting so hot in here!"

They dashed and slid behind a control panel. Blake peeked above the top. All three guards were hunched over, creeping toward them. Blake placed his hand on her knee. She was trembling. "Don't panic. You have to keep calm."

He braved a second look. The guys were closer. Blake fired four shots. One man fell. Sparks flew and the heat from the blaze grew more intense. Sofia was sweating and began to cry. "The building is going to explode! I don't want to die this way!"

He released his magazine. There was one round left, plus one in the chamber. "I'll get us out of here. We're leaving now."

Machine gun fire echoed throughout the building. Blake and Sofia ducked, but none of the bullets hit the control panel. No more shots rang out. Both had furrowed brows as they locked eyes. A familiar voice called out. "Blake! Get your ass out of there now! We have to go. Move!"

He jumped to his feet. Standing in the doorway was Solomon Zinn, a Mossad agent he knew all too well.

"Solomon?"

She waved them on. "Come on!"

Blake reached for Sofia's hand, and they all ran hard to the exit, picking up the weapons of the men Solomon shot. Everyone within the building tried to escape and paid no attention to anything or anyone. Blake, Sofia, and Solomon made it to the long hallway leading to the exit. An enormous explosion rocked the building. The concussion knocked them all to the ground. Blake raised his head as a fireball flowed toward them like a wave of water. Fear edged his voice. "Get up! Run!"

Once again, he pulled her to him. They ran as fast as their bodies would let them. The heat on their backs drove them forward as they sprinted for the door. "We're almost there!"

Bursting through the doors, they made a hard right and dove to the ground. A second later, a plume of fire blasted the doors open and spewed outside the building, followed by a plume of black smoke. They all lay on the ground, face down. Blake turned to Sofia. She smiled back. Feeling battered by the concussion, with a determined effort, he forced himself onto his knees. "Come on."

Blake stood and helped her and Solomon to their feet. They gazed out into the parking lot, where cars scattered in a wild frenzy as people tried to escape.

He faced Solomon. "What in the hell are you doing here?"

"Saving your ass before I kick it. You owe me for Vienna."

Blake stepped toward her. "I don't owe you shit! I was accomplishing my job."

Solomon pushed Blake back. "Bullshit! Fallahi was mine, and you stole him!"

He took a pace forward. "You were going to kill him. Do you—"

She pointed to herself with her thumb. "It was *my* mission! I failed!"

Blake turned away, then back. "Right, and as I was going to say; do you have any idea—any fucking idea at all—how much intel we got from him once we interrogated him? Huh? Do you?"

Blake took a moment to glance at Sofia, who was standing with her mouth agape. Not sure what to make of the exchange happening before her. He swiveled back to Solomon. "We got enough intelligence to send a successful cyber-attack, terminating their nuclear program for decades, if not permanently."

He shook his head. "Had you killed him, none of it would have been possible. They were ready to attack Israel in less than eighteen months." His jaw clenched. "And killing him would have only emboldened them and would have moved the timetable up."

Allowing her a few moments to let his words sink in was to his advantage. Her shoulders dropped and her jaw was no longer clenched. She turned away and surveyed the parking lot.

Blake allowed her a moment before he continued. "No. You didn't know, did you? Maybe you should thank me instead of berating me."

Sofia tapped Blake on the back of his arm. He snapped at her. "What?"

She flinched. "I hate to interrupt your lovely reunion, but there is a chopper coming and I think it's Petrovich."

A helicopter approached, flying close to the ground. Automatic weapon fire came from the side of the chopper. Blake dove toward Sofia and tackled her to the ground as bullets shredded the area where they once stood. Sofia rolled over and stood. She held her hand to her forehead to shade the sun. "It was Petrovich. He's headed to his airstrip.

He's going to get away."

A wry smile crept across Blake's face. "I don't think so."

#

Petrovich sat in his chopper. Looking out below, he surveyed his life's work, now a flaming carnage. Reaching for his phone, he called his pilot and told him to prepare the jet. He found something thick in his jacket pocket. He reached in and pulled out the mysterious bulge. It was a stack of thin adhesive patches. The top one had a blinking red light. He froze in place and his face turned white as the blood drained from his head.

#

Blake pulled out Lance's phone, and with the application still open, he hit send. The helicopter disintegrated into a plume of fire and smoke before it crashed to the ground. Blake turned to Sofia and smiled while she stared on in shock. Refocusing on Solomon, Blake stepped over to her. "So, what are you doing here? How did you know I was here?"

Her eyes widened. "What?" She chuckled. "Don't be so vain. I had no idea you were here." She pointed her chin toward Sofia. "I came for her."

Pointing toward herself, Sofia walked toward the two. "Me?"

"Yeah, you. You're more popular than you think."

She tilted her head to the side. "How so?"

Solomon shook her head and turned away. "You're clueless, you know that? There were four intelligence agents on the train with you and one of Petrovich's men. All following you."

Sofia covered her open mouth with her hand. "Oh, my God. I had no idea."

Solomon smiled. "Like I said. Clueless."

Blake glanced at his watch. "You can tell us once we're on the plane. I assume you're coming with us?"

"Oh no. I've still got a job to do." She slapped him on the shoulder. "And you should help me."

"What is it?"

She clapped her hands. "You don't know, do you?"

Blake's jaw tensed, and his eyes narrowed. "Solomon? What aren't you telling me?"

"Well, oh my. Mr. Big Shot, the secret agent, doesn't know about the bioweapons he was developing."

"Bioweapons? No. This is the first I've heard!"

He turned to Sofia. "Did you know anything about this?"

Shaking her head, she turned away, then back. "No. Never. I had no idea he was involved in bioweapons research."

The smile left Solomon's face. "Petrovich was following his admiration for creating disasters and thought of a new idea. He's been doing gain-of-function research on several viruses and came up with a doozy. His plan was to release it, let it kill a few million people and then, of course—miraculously, be the first to develop a vaccine. He'd sell billions of vaccines to every country in the world. It would make him the world's first trillionaire."

"How'd Mossad find out?"

Solomon shook her head. "Oh no. I'm not giving you that information."

Blake put his hands on his hips and thought for a moment. "Okay." He nodded. "Let's do it. Where are they?"

"Okay, come on. They're in the building over there. I'll tell you on the way."

22

Petrovich Research Facility
Eastern Siberia, Russia
December 22nd
11:25 (03:07 GMT)

#

The three entered the bioengineering building. Blake checked his weapon. Solomon nodded to him. "What have you got left?"

"Nearly a full mag here for the MP5. I've got only two rounds in my Glock."

Solomon reached for her backpack hanging from one shoulder and unzipped it. "What is it? Seventeen?"

"Of course."

She sniggered. "Typical CIA. So predictable." She rummaged in her bag and handed him two spare 9mm mags for his pistol. Putting the pack back over her shoulders, she smirked. "I keep adding to all the shit you're going to owe me for."

"Yeah?" Blake peeked around the corner. "Remind me to write you an IOU. There are two armed men guarding the lab."

Sofia cleared her throat. "What is it with you two? The gas line supplying the other building also supplies this one. We're lucky if we have five minutes."

Blake turned to her. "There will be emergency cut-off valves. They should shut off the flow automatically. But it doesn't mean the fire won't spread over here. My question is, with all the commotion going on outside, why aren't they evacuating? Do you know where they would keep this stuff?"

Sofia shook her head. "I don't know. And no, but the guards will have key cards to gain entry to the laboratory. I'm afraid I'm not familiar with the layout of the place or—"

Solomon interrupted. "I do. I've seen a detailed schematic. Inside the laboratory is another locked one with an airlock for access. It's got to be where they're storing the weapon. And they're probably getting all the samples out now so they can evacuate, so we have to stop waiting around and move. Now."

She reached into her backpack and withdrew a small container. "This box will store two vials: one virus and one antidote. It will keep them at minus one hundred degrees, but only for eight hours. I must transfer them to another freezer before then."

"So, how do we get into the airlock? Do you have any ideas?" She glanced at Sofia.

"The technicians inside should have a key card."

Solomon chambered a round in the other MP5. "I say we go shoot the sentries. Let's go."

Sofia lifted her hands. "No. Wait. I have an idea. You two be ready."

She walked around the corner with a sense of urgency and called out to the guards.

"You two. Come here. I want your help."

The two men turned to each other, then back to Sofia. "Come on!" She raised her arm and pointed. "Can't you hear the commotion outside? The compound is on fire. I'm asking you to find the central gas valve and turn it off." She waved them to her. "Come quick. Now!"

Sofia returned, sighed, and then gestured to the others. "Both of you, get ready."

He put his back to the wall and listened. The pounding of their feet came closer. He timed it perfectly so as the guard turned the corner, Blake slammed him in the forehead with the butt of his rifle.

His head snapped back, then landed with a thud, striking the back of his head against the tiles. The other raised his weapon while Solomon fired three rounds into his chest. Empty shells from the MP5 danced on the floor like tiny bells. He picked the access card off the dead man's belt.

"Let's go."

They entered the lab. The two agents had their weapons drawn. A middle-aged woman with curly blonde hair past her shoulders glanced toward them in shock. Her eyes were magnified by the thick lenses of her gold-framed glasses. Solomon approached her. "Hands."

Giving no resistance, the woman raised her arms. "What's going on? Who are you? What do you want?"

Solomon's eyes focused on the name printed across her badge. "Gerta? I'll make this as simple as I can. Do you have access to the virus and antidote in the air-locked chamber?"

Her enlarged eyes blinked, then shifted to the left. "Uhhh…"

The barrel of the MP5 lifted toward the ceiling, and Solomon squeezed the trigger. The woman flinched and closed her eyes. Dust from the tiles above settled on her head and shoulders. The shaking in her voice revealed her fear. "Yes. Okay!"

"Fantastic. You and I are going to go in there and you're going to give me a sample of each. Got it?"

Gerta pointed to the biosafety suits hanging on the wall. "We have to wear the hazmat gear."

Solomon motioned with the barrel of her firearm for Greta to step over to the suits. After the scientist had put on her protective clothing, Solomon handed her weapon to Blake and donned her hazmat suit.

They taped the seams at their wrists, ankles and neck and proceeded into the airlock, and then the sealed room storing the samples Solomon needed. Sofia reached out to Blake and placed her hand on his arm. "Who is this woman, and how do you know her?"

Releasing a deep sigh, Blake moved toward the window and peered out. "She and I worked on a case a few years ago. It was a credit card cloning scheme in the Middle East. Some terrorist organizations used them to fund their twisted cause. The assignment was a successful venture between the CIA and Mossad."

He sighed. "It was when we teamed well together. However, more recently, I had a mission to grab someone we identified as a potential asset so we could interrogate him for intel. They assigned her to kill him. So, the whole time, we were adversaries. I ended up with the man and she had to go home, failing at her task."

"And was it the Fallahi who she spoke about earlier?"

Nodding, Blake turned and stepped toward her. "Yeah. He was in charge of Iran's nuclear program. He'd been hiding and kept himself off the grid for seven years. We thought he was dead. There were some leadership changes in Iran and, unexpectedly, he reappeared and announces he was going back to head their nuclear research. For us, it was a chance to grab him."

An annoyed expression briefly crossed his face. "We could finally get an accurate assessment of where Iran was with their nuclear program. This guy was Iran's Oppenheimer, a real nuclear guru, and Mossad saw him as a major threat, and this was their chance to take him out." Blake chuckled. "And—there was a terrorist cell out of Libya rebuilding themselves after Benghazi and they—"

Blake shook his head and smiled. "They saw it as an opportunity to kidnap him for ransom and use the money to get back in the terrorist business. So, it was a bunch of fun trying to fight those assholes while avoiding her sights. And she's a damn fine shot, too."

"Why do I get the sense there was something between you two?"

Blake smiled and laughed. "Us?" He smirked while he shook his head. "Ah, well, perhaps a long time ago."

Sofia stepped close to Blake and reached for his hand. "And now?"

Blake released her hand and shook his head. "No. The last time she saw me, she tried to kill me, so…"

An explosion rocked the building and rattled the windows. Both Blake and Sofia rushed to the window. A huge fireball was stretching to the sky from below ground. The white and gray plume of smoke swirling above. "That's not what we want to see."

"Blake, what is it?"

Another explosion rocked the building. The result was another fireball coming from the ground, but closer.

"It's emanating from the gas line buried between these two buildings. The cutoffs must have failed. We don't have much time."

He ran over to the sealed room, tapped on the glass, and yelled at Solomon. "We have to go!"

Solomon pointed to her head and shook it from side to side. He searched for an intercom or some way to communicate with her. Sofia called out. "There." She gestured to a mic on the side of the wall. Grabbing it, he pressed the button. "Can you hear me?"

She nodded.

"The gas cut-off valves have failed, and this building is going to blow. We gotta go."

After she acknowledged, he went to every station and turned on the gas feeding the Bunsen burners. Next, he found some batteries and wrapped them in aluminum foil and placed them in a microwave.

Sofia was staring out the window when another fireball blew from the ground. "It's getting closer! What are you doing?"

"I have to make sure those virus samples get destroyed. This is a little insurance policy."

Solomon opened the outside door of the airlock. "Okay, I got what I needed. Let's—"

The concussion wave blew glass throughout the laboratory. Sofia brushed off her sleeves and started for the door. Blake dashed over to the microwave as Gerta was leaving the room. He set the timer for 5 minutes and hit start. Out in the hall were other people, all running for the exits. Some were standing, looking around, confused. He waved his arms at them. "Go! Go! Go!"

They rounded the corner when a blast blew the lab door off its hinges. Blake stopped and felt for a pulse of the guard he knocked out. "Sofia! Solomon! Come!" He motioned them back. "He's still alive. Help me get him outside."

They carried him and laid him in the grass. Blake placed his hands on his hips and took a few deep breaths and nodded to Solomon. "Did you get what you needed?"

Catching her breath, she was bent over with her hands on her knees. "Yeah. I did."

Another explosion shook the ground. The roof of the lab blew off. Parts of the building rained over them, and they all ran into the parking lot, ducking to avoid getting hit by the flying debris. Solomon checked the seal of her container. Once satisfied the seal was safe, she put it in her backpack. "I don't suppose you have a fast way outta here, do you?"

He chuckled. "Of course. We're going to take his jet."

A smile creased her lips. "I like it!"

A motorcar came at them, driving away from the melee. Blake pointed his pistol at the front windshield. Brakes screeched as it ground to a halt. He opened the door. A wiry, short man wearing a lab coat darkened from the fire and smoke turned his head to him. Blake grabbed his arm. "You can drive us to the airfield, or you can get out here and I'm taking your vehicle. Your choice."

The man nodded his agreement, and all three rode to the airstrip where the jet waited for Petrovich. The automobile stopped right next to the plane. They quickly ascended the stairs and Blake went straight to the cockpit, pointing his pistol at the pilot. "Both of you. Out now."

The men raised their hands. The two exchanged glances and went back to Blake. "We have to wait for—"

"He's dead. Trust me, he won't be making this flight." He then pointed to the co-pilot. "You. Out."

The man protested. "But—"

Blake grabbed him by the collar and jerked him out of his seat. He pulled him through the cabin door and toward the aircraft's opening. The man continued to argue. "What are you doing?"

"What part of *out* don't you understand?" He released his grip and delivered a kick, sending him tumbling onto the tarmac. The engines were starting when he returned to the cockpit. "Now your turn."

The pilot raised both hands. "Who's going to fly the plane?"

Solomon stepped near the door. "I am. Now get out now before I shoot you."

The pilot exited, and Blake raised the stairs and closed the door. After taking off, the jet ascended to its cruising altitude of forty-thousand feet. Solomon got on the intercom and asked for a destination.

Blake went to the cockpit and opened the door. "Head west toward Germany. Let me make a few calls and determine where the best place would be to handle your payload and keep it safe."

"Correct MacKay. It's *my* cargo. It's part of my mission and you'd better not fuck it up."

Blake shut the door and sat near Sofia. Turning on the plane's radio, he dialed in a U.S. Military frequency. After identifying himself, he explained the situation. He received permission to proceed to Ramstein Air Force Base in Germany.

Blake breathed a sigh of relief. "Okay, now all the commotion is over, we can sit back and relax." He went back and told Solomon their destination. Then, he strolled to the bar, where he picked out a bottle of champagne and two glasses. He brought them over to Sofia, who lay stretched out on the leather couch. Blake opened the bottle.

"I'm going to go to the restroom and freshen up." She leaned in and kissed him on the cheek.

He smiled. "Take your time."

"Wait!"

He set the bottle on the table and stood. He approached her, reached around, and placed his hand on her butt. Blake pulled her close to him. They passionately kissed for a minute. Their eyes met as they pulled apart. Both with broad grins. "Okay, now you can go. You're kind of stinky anyhow?"

She laughed. "Ha! Now see if you get lucky."

Blake chuckled along. He grabbed the champagne as he sat and started to pour.

She opened the restroom door and let out a scream. A gunshot rang out, and Sofia fell to the floor. Blake jumped to his feet. Vasily emerged out of the doorway and pointed his pistol at Blake.

Blake focused on Sofia. She'd been shot through her right clavicle; painful for sure, but not fatal. But he needed to stop the bleeding and keep her from going into shock. He raised his hands in front of him. "Now, Vasily. Vasily, right?"

The man said nothing.

"You know you can't fire a gun in here. If it punctures the outside of the jet, we all die."

"Worked fine a second ago."

The aircraft rumbled with some slight turbulence.

"Listen. Your boss is dead. You have nothing to gain by killing us."

The plane shook again, but harder. They both lost their balance. Blake grabbed the seat next to him, pushed himself off at his adversary and grasped the arm holding the firearm. Vasily fired twice. The bullets ripped through the floor. Blake spun around and elbowed Vasily in the face and flipped him over onto the floor. Cabin alarms blared. Blake turned to the cockpit. "Descend! Descend!"

"What the hell is going on back there?"

The airplane started to descend. Blake jumped on his opponent but was met with a foot to the gut.

He fell back onto the couch. Vasily aimed his pistol at him. The champagne bottle rocked back and forth on the couch as the golden liquid flowed from the top. Blake grabbed it and threw it at his assailant. The weapon discharged another round, tearing through the window. The cabin depressurized as the window blew out, alarms screamed, and the aircraft went into a steep dive. "I can't control it!"

Gravity had slammed Vasily onto the ceiling of the cabin. Blake fought against it and held tight to the bottom of the couch. It was too much force. Blake let gravity take control of his body and slammed into Vasily as the plane went down.

He pulled out his knife and swung toward Vasily's arm. The Russian screamed in pain and released the weapon. Blake drove his fist hard three times into his attacker's face. The Russian fought back hard with a knee to Blake's groin.

Blake held steady through the pain. He ripped the knife from Vasily's arm and slashed hard toward the burly man's chest. Vasily raised his other arm in defense and blocked the knife from its intended target. Both men struggled against each other, testing their strength.

Blake reached around to his left ankle and pulled another blade. He drove it deep into the left side of Vasily's torso. His eyes widened with shock. His strength weakened. Blake moved his left hand to the other knife and with both hands drove the blade through Vasily's chest.

He turned, desperate to find Sofia. The G-force of the plunging jet pressed her body against the ceiling. She was out cold. Blood bubbled from the Russian's mouth. He removed the blade from Vasily's side and plunged it deep into his heart. Blake bore witness as the life in the Russian's eyes faded away.

Solomon begged from the front of the plane. "I need help!"

The small aircraft shook violently as it leveled out. Vasily, Blake and Sofia all fell to the plane's floor. Blake fought his way through the continued turbulence back to Sofia's unconscious form.

He checked her pulse, lifted her into his arms, and secured her in a seat. He stumbled to the cockpit, falling into the co-pilot's place. After fastening his belt. Blake grabbed his yoke to assist. Solomon still battled to gain control of the jet.

The plane had descended from forty-thousand feet to twenty-two thousand feet in thirty seconds. Both struggled against the force working against them. At fifteen thousand feet, they regained control of the jet. At twelve thousand feet, they could feel the pressure leveling inside the cabin.

Blake and Solomon turned to each other. Both took deep breaths. "Can you handle it now?" Blake jerked his thumb toward the back of the aircraft. "She took one in the shoulder, and I have to check on her."

"Yes, but we have another problem." Solomon pointed to several lights on the dash. "Look here. We have no hydraulics for the landing gear. We can't land."

"You allow me to worry about that. Send out a mayday and tell everyone our new altitude. Keep the path clear." She nodded, and he went to the back of the aircraft.

Sofia was pressing on her wound. Blake grabbed a bottle of vodka and some towels. "This is going to hurt." He poured the vodka on her injury. Her jaw clenched when she closed her eyes tight. She moaned through gritted teeth. Blake checked her back. "I need you to lean forward."

He examined the back of her shoulder. "You have no exit wound. The bullet is still in there. Don't worry, you'll be ok. We have to stop the bleeding, though." He handed her the towel. "Keep applying pressure. I've got to get us off this plane."

23

10,000 ft above the Baltic Sea
　12:45 (10:15 GMT)
　December 22nd

#

The C-130 glided in and held steady two hundred meters off the damaged jet's port side. In response to Blake's request for assistance, the Swedish Navy directed them out over the Baltic. He was on the radio with the pilot of the cargo plane. "We're holding level and ready to receive."

"Roger. Sending the line now."

Unexpectedly, Solomon yelled out from the cockpit's open door. "Hey, get in here!"

He pressed his mic button. "SE fourteen zero four. Standby."

As he entered the cockpit, she turned to him. "We have a problem. I'm getting all kinds of chatter on the squawk box about some bad turbulence at this altitude."

After a deep sigh and a glance out the windscreen, he saw the C-130 keeping steady. "How long?"

She shook her head. "A minute. Perhaps two."

He placed his hand on her shoulder. "All right. I have faith in you. Hold this damn thing tight."

She nodded, refocused out the front, and gripped the yoke with both hands. He exited the cockpit and went to the back and pulled out a duffle while he radioed the C-130. "SE fourteen zero four. We're getting reports of turbulence in the area. Can you confirm? Over."

"Uh, affirmative. We need to do this now. Over."

"Copy. I'm opening the door now."

Blake took the black webbing he retrieved from the bag and tied it into a makeshift harness. With the remaining length, he made a short tether and attached one end to his himself and clipped the other to a handle inside the fuselage with a carabiner. He released the door lever and gripped it tight. "Sofia, be prepared. The wind in here is about to be terrific."

The aircraft shuddered. She plopped herself into the seat and struggled with her seatbelt. Blake noticed her wince in pain as she buckled the belt.

"Do you need help?"

Shaking her head, she winced as the buckle snapped. "No, I've got it."

"Okay, are you ready?"

She nodded. When the door opened, the cabin filled with a constant rush of wind. He gazed out the window at the C-130. Clipped to a black nylon rope, a carabiner exited from the lowered rear hatch. The rope swayed in the turbulent air. He pressed the radio's transmit button. "You'll have to ascend and move to the right two degrees."

The rope got closer as the other pilot followed Blake's instructions. "I need a little more slack."

Two feet from the door, the metal clip clanged on the outside. "A little more, if you've got it."

Suddenly, the rope was thirty feet away. Blake noticed the C-130 lurch hard and gain altitude; its wings flapping from the turbulence and then it struck them. The heavy rocking threw him into the wooden cabinet on the other side of the fuselage. The craft shuttered violently. "We've hit the turbulence. I'm trying to hold it steady!"

The jet lurched up as it gained altitude. A second later, they felt as if they were in a freefall, losing over two hundred feet in a few seconds. Blake's body slammed into the ceiling. Alarms blared from up in front. Sofia screamed. The engines' screams and whines infiltrated the open cabin, along with the wind. "Blake!"

The aircraft righted itself, and he found himself on the floor. It smoothed out. He was wide-eyed and his breathing heavy. "Is that it?

Are we done?"

Solomon's voice came from the cockpit. "I don't know. Better get seated until we know for sure. Hurry."

He stumbled to his feet. "This is the fucking worst flight I've ever—"

The plane lurched to the left and bumped hard, flinging him out the open door. The rope snapped tight. Blake's body slammed into the fuselage. He turned and saw Sofia through the window, panicking. He couldn't hear her screams. A quick glance behind him. His feet were only inches away from the whirring engine's blades.

He pulled on the tether and slowly battled along his way to the door's opening. With each pull, the muscles in his arms burned. The leveling out brought him a much-needed sense of relief. Right over left, he inched himself to the door.

He was within a grasp of the door. He reached out with his hand and got a fingertip in the doorway. The plane lurched. He lost his grip and fell back. They lost altitude. It bobbed again. He felt closer to the engine than before. His harness had loosened.

The painful ascent back to the open door was once again underway. His arms were on fire. Three or four inches at a time. He was less than a foot from the door and he jerked back again. He could see inside. His makeshift anchor was tearing from the fuselage.

"Oh, shit!" Blake pulled hard and fast. Eight inches to go. Four. One. The handle snapped. Two sets of hands reached out and grabbed his arms. Sofia and Solomon heaved him into the plane. Sofia got on her knees and embraced him. "Oh, my God! Are you all right?"

He took in a few deep breaths and started laughing. "Ooooh, holy shit!" He continued to laugh. "Oh, my God." He stood up and pointed to Solomon. "That sucked!"

She smiled enthusiastically. "Yes. It did. But we're out of it now. And now you owe me your life." She smirked before returning to the cockpit. He clapped his hands. "Okay! Let's try this again. I need you to sit down and buckle up."

Getting on the radio, he communicated with the Swedes and lined up the C-130 again. As previously, a long line came from the back, but unlike the previous attempt, it crept perfectly to a few inches outside the open doorway. Reaching out, he grasped the rope and attached it to another grip. "Got it. Send the chutes."

The C-130 ascended to increase the angle of the tether. He watched as two parachutes descended, one for Solomon and another, outfitted with a tandem harness, for him and Sofia. He grabbed both chutes and placed them in the front seat. As a last task, he unclipped the carabiner and let it fly loose. "Package received. Thanks."

"Roger. Best of luck."

The other pilot took a sharp turn in the opposite direction. As the Swedish Saab JAS 39 Gripen fighter jet closed in behind them, Blake turned to the south. He changed channels to speak with his pilot. "We're in business, but I've got some bad news."

"What do you mean, *bad news*?"

"When I asked about a facility to store your samples, it got out they were viral biohazards."

Waiting for some kind of response, the tone wasn't friendly when it came. "And?"

"They aren't equipped with anything to hold them safely and we can't go to an installation able to accommodate them in a reasonable amount of time. They can't risk it getting out."

There was no answer. "I'm sorry, Solomon."

He turned to Sofia. She shrugged. "Once we are clear, they'll shoot the plane down, so the wreckage—and the samples—get incinerated and fall into the sea rather than a populated area."

"God dammit, MacKay!"

Her voice boomed through the plane's intercom and spilled out from the closed cockpit door. He squinted and cringed as she spoke. "Here we go again. You fucked me the last time, and you're fucking me this time. I swear to God, I hope I never see you on another fucking mission as long as I live."

The line went quiet. He put the mic to his mouth. "Are you finished?"

After not hearing, he went to the cockpit and opened the door. "Hey, are you ready for this?"

She handed him the vial container. "Yes, but we have to go now! We're now less than fifteen miles from the shoreline."

"Okay, we only have a couple of minutes. Come now."

Solomon set the plane to autopilot to keep it steady and raced into the main cabin. Seizing one of the parachutes, she put it on and waited for Blake's signal. Putting on his parachute, he hurried to Sofia.

Grabbing the vodka bottle, he held it toward her with a grin. "I suggest you take a few gulps of this."

"Why?"

"Because the straps of your harness will press against your wound and it will hurt like hell."

She snatched the bottle, took two big swigs, and poured more on her gunshot. She reached for her injury; her face crumpled in agony, like an old pumpkin left for weeks after Halloween. She swore in a Russian dialect he didn't understand. "I know it hurts, but we've got to get out now!"

Blake helped her into the tandem straps and was gentle with the part covering her bloody shoulder.

"Dammit, it hurts. Hold on!" Sofia grabbed the vodka and took another gulp. "Ok. Let's get this done."

He handed her a small earpiece and a throat mic. "Here, wear this. It will allow us to communicate as we're falling."

"You'll be right behind me. I'll hear you, won't I?"

"No. Just put it on and—"

"This is JAS seventy- seven. You have thirty seconds. Over."

He put his hand over his ear. "Come back? I didn't hear you."

"You have less than thirty seconds before we shoot you down. You need to exit immediately. Over."

"Roger. We're heading to the door now."

He reached under Sofia's legs and picked her up. He staggered to the door. Blake nodded at Solomon. Without hesitation, she flipped him her middle finger and jumped out backward. The fighter pilot squawked on the radio again. "You have ten seconds before I fire. Over."

Adrenaline pumped through his body as he counted to three. "Ready?"

Sofia had her eyes closed tight. "No, but do it so we—"

As the exhilarating rush of wind enveloped them, he fearlessly propelled them into the open sky, embracing the adrenaline coursing through his veins. She released a shrill scream, a testament to the fear pulsing through her being. The air rushed past them as they accelerated.

All sense of falling melted away as they reached terminal velocity. The JAS Gripen fired its AIM-9 Sidewinder missiles. They slammed into the jet's fuselage and detonated. He witnessed the flaming inferno as it dove and crashed into the Baltic Sea. "Do you see the ship down there?"

"No!"

"Open your eyes."

Sofia pushed past the fear and forced her eyelids open. "Yes, I see it now. The water is getting closer. Real fast. Are you going to pull the cord?"

"I will. I want you to enjoy the view."

"Okay, I enjoyed it. Now pull the damn cord."

"All right, but remember, it's going to hurt like hell."

"Pull the goddamn cord!"

Blake yanked the release handle. The straps gripped her body as they decelerated from two-hundred kilometers per hour to a slow descent of thirty kilometers per hour almost immediately. The three and a half Gs pressed hard on Sofia's wound. As if someone parked a car on her clavicle and turned the wheels back and forth for good measure.

The pain was so intense she felt lightheaded, and darkness crept in, but subsided as fast as it came. Blake released her seconds prior to splashing down into the sea. She screamed the entire fall. Sofia hit the water moments before Blake. When he surfaced, she yelled at him. "Why the hell did you drop me?"

"So we wouldn't get tangled in the parachute lines and drown. I figured you wouldn't mind."

"You could have told me."

"Would it have made any difference?"

She said nothing. He smirked. "That's what I thought."

The Zodiac slowed next to her. Two men reached and pulled her into the boat. Solomon was already sitting with a towel wrapped around her. He trod water while waiting. "Careful, she's wounded—stray bullet."

"I'll radio the ship and have a medical team stand by."

Epilogue

Stockholm, Sweden
    December 24th
    14:30 (13:30 GMT)

#

Blake walked into the physical therapy wing of the *Ersta sjukhus* hospital. His dark wool overcoat swayed with each step. The huge stuffed elephant and an enormous bouquet of roses covered his face. He checked in with the front desk and they directed him to this area. Sofia had undergone surgery and spent the last couple of days recovering. Today was her first day of therapy.

When he entered the room, she was lying on a table, flat on her chest. A therapist wearing green scrubs with SpongeBob SquarePants on them was holding Sofia's arm.

She was doing exercises for her rotator cuff with her right arm hanging over the side. The nurse turned to him and he put a finger to his lips. She smiled and nodded, then told Sofia to do five more repetitions, then stepped out of the room to give him privacy.

Sofia halted her reps and turned her head, feeling the softness of the vinyl padding brush against her cheek. She widened her eyes and beamed a smile at the sight of Blake and the beautiful flowers before her. Struggling to sit up, she reached for him. He grasped her hands to help her up. He leaned into her embrace.

"Oh, you are a sight for sore eyes. Thank you for coming."

He was careful not to hug her too hard. "I couldn't stay away. I'm glad you're making a recovery. You seem to be doing all right."

"I am. It still hurts like hell, but this is my first day. It will get better." She squeezed him tight.

"Ahhh, you're squeezing me to death." She let up. Blake pulled back, and they laughed together. "I'm sure it will. One thing I've learned about recovering is *do your therapy*. The more you do it, the faster you'll heal."

They stared into each other's eyes for a moment. She didn't need to say anything. He could sense how she felt. He broke the silence.

"So, listen. I've talked with my people back in D.C. and I can get you into the country on an extended visa if you want to. I don't know if you've reflected on what you'll do next."

Sofia smiled. "Well, lying in bed all day gave me time to think. I made a few calls yesterday evening. My former Cambridge Professor has a lot of pull. He is creating a position for me there. I have a bunch of old friends still in the area and I'm familiar with it, so…"

Blake nodded. "That's impressive. I think you'll be happy there."

She placed her palm on his chest. "So what's happened in the past couple of days?"

"You don't want to know. The Swedes weren't ecstatic about downing the plane. They're not a NATO member and there are some bullshit politics involved. The politicians can sort it out, though. It's not my problem."

"What about the array? Did you get your missing operative?"

"The Russians deny they ever knew it, which is total crap. So, to maintain the whole *'we didn't know anything'* charade, they've cooperated and allowed a team to help with the clean-up. They have also retrieved Agent Tucker's body. He is on his way back home now."

"And what about Solomon? Did she get back to Israel?"

Blake rubbed the back of his neck. With some hesitation, he answered. "Uh, No. She's outside in the car. I'm giving her a ride to the airport."

Disappointment etched across her face and her gaze drifted to the floor. "I see. Have you made up with her?"

He laughed. "I don't have an issue with her. Well—aside from her almost killing me. She's the one who has a problem with me. And if and when she gets over it—who knows?"

Sofie's eyes wandered away, then back. "And you?"

He sighed. "Back to the grind, I suppose. I fly out in a few hours."

Her voice softened. "I see." She lowered her chin and twiddled her fingers.

Despite feeling for Sofia, Blake knew their paths were not meant to converge. He was flying back to D.C. and she was starting a new life for herself in England. He lifted her chin with his right hand and gazed at her. Her eyes glistened as tears formed in the corners. A lone drop fell from her cheek.

"Take care of yourself. You're a tough woman." He leaned in and kissed her on the lips.

Sofia's voice trailed off as she responded. "You too, my hero."

He turned and left the room. He could feel her eyes on him as he walked away, his thoughts consumed by the thoughts of what might have been.

#

Blake left the hospital and made his way back to his car. As he approached, he didn't see Solomon in the front seat. He scanned the area but didn't see any sign of her. For all he knew, she could be bearing down on him through the scope of her rifle.

As he opened the door, he saw a yellow handwritten message sitting in the middle of the dash.

I decided to take a different flight. Take care of yourself, MacKay. If I see you again, it'll be too soon.

Blake chuckled to himself, then wadded up the note and tossed it in the back seat. When he started the car, his encrypted phone rang. It was Mike, his handler.

"Blake. Where the hell are you?"

"Stockholm."

"You're not on the fucking plane? I need you back here. We've got something brewing."

He shifted the vehicle into drive. "What is it this time?"

"Let's just say you should brush up on your Spanish. Cuban would be best. We may want you to take someone out. But they're difficult to get close to. Well guarded."

"Ha. You don't know me too well then. Sounds simple."

Mike's tone turned to one Blake seldom heard. His voice was grave. "This will be the deepest and longest undercover assignment you've done. Be prepared."

Mike ended the call.

#

Solomon sat in the back of the cab, looking out over the water at the colorful cruise ships docked when her phone rang. The number was private, but she knew who it was.

"Yes?"

"I assume you are on your way home?"

"Yes."

"And do you have them?"

She reached into her backpack and retrieved an identical storage case from the one she was told to leave on the plane. She opened the top to reveal the two vials she took from the lab.

"Safe and secure."

END

Other titles by this author:
    Novellas;
    Intercept
    Novels;
    Spear Garden
    Deep Rising (Coming 2025)

* 9 7 8 1 0 8 8 2 5 0 2 3 5 *